The R

The Road to Brightcity
Máirtín Ó Cadhain

POOLBEG

First published 1981 by
Poolbeg Press Ltd.
Knocksedan House,
Swords, Co. Dublin, Ireland.
This edition published 1987

With acknowledgements to An Gúm, publishers of *Idir Shúgradh agus Dáiríre* (1939) and *An Braon Broghach* (1948) by Máirtín O Cadhain, from which collections the stories translated in this book are taken.

Cover illustration by Robert Ballagh
Designed by Stephen Hope
Printed by The Guernsey Press Co. Ltd.,
Vale, Guernsey, Channel Islands.

Contents

Introduction

Mairtin O Cadhain was born, 1906, in Cois Fharraige, that part of the Connemara littoral flanking Galway Bay. Cut off from the rest of Ireland by great mountain ranges and lakes, and psychologically cut off by its own Irish language and culture, preserved there as in a fortress, it had for more than a century looked west across the Atlantic to America as the nearest land, its nearest kin, its only hope.

He was of the people — 'a race', he described it in *The Year 1912*, 'whose guardian angel was the American trunk, whose guiding star was the exile ship, whose Red Sea was the Atlantic.' And of the young girl in the same story — 'she had been nurtured on American lore from infancy. South Boston, Norwood, Butte, Montana, Minnesota, California, plucked chords in her imagination more distinctly than did Dublin, Belfast, Wexford, or even places only a few miles out on the Plain beyond Brightcity.'

A scholarship to the Teachers' Training College in Dublin saved him from the exile ship. He returned, 1926, to teach in the tiny schools of the West. A young man of powerful physique and tremendous energy, naive, witty, imaginative, he was an inspiring teacher. But he was shocked by what he saw. After the long struggle for Independence and the neurotic civil war which followed, the new Irish Government was wholly unable to supply the dynamic thinking necessary to save the Cois Fharraige 'American Strip' and all the other Irish-speaking strips from North to South along the Atlantic coast. They would have preferred to forget their existence. But O Cadhain was not the forgetting kind. Seeing that the fight for Ireland, economic and psychological, must still continue, he joined the outlawed I.R.A. His republicanism was of the positive kind, with two primary objects: to check the physical erosion of a people who by then were going by whole households to America; and to check the even more terrible erosion of a mind and a culture, one of the oldest in Europe, which he saw on the brink of extinction.

1936, for his subversive activities, he was dismissed from his post as a National Teacher by the clerical management and blacklisted. During World War Two the State had him interned in the Curragh Camp, the Irish Siberia. He conducted classes in the Irish language, culture and literature among the internees, and in his enforced idleness read widely in the Celtic languages, and in English, French, German, and some Russian.

Behind barbed wire he began to develop his own particular kind of Irish short story — influenced in one direction by Gorki, to deal with aspects of the Cois Fharraige life he knew — but determined to preserve the peculiar insights from medieval and even pre-Christian times which had survived in the folk memory. One feels a certain exultation of spirit in his 1948 collection of stories: the born teacher discovering himself as the born writer.

In the late forties he found employment in the Government Translation Department, but he still continued the economic and cultural fight. As a freelance journalist he shaped a vitriolic style, using the most shattering idioms of the living Irish speech laced with phrases from the seventeenth century literature and new coinages from the thinking of Darwin, Einstein and Freud, in pamphlets, articles, letters, lampoons, striking blindly at all sides, hurting even friends to his cause whom he considered lax or lukewarm, attacking the dehumanising of life and the castration of culture with a blistering invective and a scurrility unsurpassed since Swift.

Trinity College, Dublin, recognising his scholarship and his service to the nation, gave him a post as lecturer and later as professor in their Irish Department. But though he took up the teaching with zest he never became *embourgeoisé*. To his own people he was still plain 'Mairtin', still learning from them, still in the forefront of every battle, in the thick of every dogfight, and on every available platform agitating for their civil rights and the survival of their tongue. And still the *enfant terrible* of Irish letters. At his death in 1970, the man was already a myth.

2.

O Cadhain the creative writer comes as a surprise. In his stories there is none of the violence and aggression which marked his public life. He is too fine an artist to attribute his own seething sense of injustice to his characters who, for the most part, are patient and longsuffering, struggling with their own immemorial way of life and detached from the political world. His delineations are delicately studied and finely rounded out, grim, comic, caustic, lyrical, heroic, compassionate. With one breathtaking novel and six collections of short stories, the last published posthumously in 1977, he made an outstanding contribution to Irish writing and to its extension as a means of presenting the complexities of the human spirit in its material milieu. 'As Maurice has *les Landes*, so O Cadhain has Cois Fharraige.' —Maire Mhac a' tSaoi.

The nine stories rendered in this book are set back in time between 1900 and 1920. The people he presents are survivors, remnants of a Celtic civilisation that had been pushed ever farther towards the western seaboard by succeeding waves of English-speaking peoples. They have lost everything, forgotten by history, and still sunk in a serf-like medieval economy, they are barely clinging to life on bog, stony garth, mountain pasture and shore. But they have preserved almost intact the riches of an ancient language which had been subject to centuries of literary development in fiction, poetry, satire, social and metaphysical thinking.

The people depicted are, blessedly, no saints. Friendly, hospitable, witty and wayward, fond of music and merry-making, they can be mean, crude, sly, stupid, pugnacious and puritanical. And just like the rest of us, their long-remembering is more often than not a wrong-remembering. And the first thing that strikes us about their language is that it is plain, straightforward, and down to earth. At its worst dreary, with straggles of hackneyed phrases limping the length of a page. At its best subtle, sinewy, unobtrusive, modern in every sense.

But in emphasising the plain and wellmannered style of Irish there are two reservations to be made. In the first place, the people in O Cadhain's youth had retained the habit of taking pleasure in language. Speech was one of their pastimes. Many of them, men and women, were artists in words, delighting in making fresh combinations and minting fresh images drawn from sea, sky, mountain, legend, and the details of crafts and daily work. They transcended the drudgery of daily life in song, verse, sharp saying, and 'the wild oats of speech'. In writing, this often runs riot in a verbal extravanganza, and men have been known to write whole books about little or nothing. O Cadhain spent much of his creative life in an attempt to master this extravagant urge and to harmonise it with the plain commonsense that was equally part of his heritage. A nice accommodation of the two may be seen in *The Withering Branch*.

In the second place, their plain style often masks a profundity. The real difficulty of the tongue, and its prime attraction for a modern writer, is its unique mixture of the muck-and-tangle of earth existence with a cosmic view and a sense of 'otherworld'. This otherworld sense as O Cadhain presents it is a very complex combination of a fundamentalist Christianity, emphasising the Fall of Man, with a large share of the old pagan nature religion. 'Ghost', 'phantom', 'fairy', 'the dead', 'the changeling', are practically identical terms, and all of them, along with the living, are implicated in a conflict of good and evil, light and dark. Such a worldview is the opposite of romantic, for in it almost all aspects of wild nature — not only sea and storm, but the blue sky, the butterfly, the fine-weather sparkles on the water, the hazelnuts — are felt as hostile, always inhuman, at times malicious. Among the few friendly forces are eggs, fire, greying hair and, oddly enough, hendirt.

In this milieu many things are 'alive' — the thornbush, the filling tide, the wind through the telegraph wires. This Irish double-view, a two-light of the mind, is most readily seen in the images, some extended into epic similes which are mini-stories in themselves, as when Brid in *The Road to Brightcity* sees the dusky moon, adulterated in some primordial tragedy, declining over the sea as a dying Cleopatra. Often these images are contracted into short phrases which express many areas of experience and intuition in one — for instance, the afterlife, the grim graveyard, and the little stonewalled garths of their daily struggle, are all apprehended in the witty image 'na críocha déanacha', 'the final fields'.

Life as revealed in this double focus is grim, but not tragic in the Greek sense nor absurd in the modern sense. Its central idea is action. Brid walks the nine miles barefoot carrying her load. 'Action is passion, and the passion is itself the meaning.' And there is always a sense of salvation implicit in the most dire situation if it can be grotesquely glimpsed as 'deonú Dé', 'God's gift', and one blindly, insanely even, carries on.

In this language and its art forms, interpenetrating the naive and the commonplace, there has always been present some dark, disjointed, manic intuition of reality which disconcerts a reader who had imagined Irish to be merely quaint, whimsical, an escape into fantasy. It is like being confronted with a Rouault *Christ* where one had expected to see a Jack B. Yeats *Blackbird Bathing in Tir-na-nOg*.

Certain critics have compared O Cadhain in Irish to Joyce in English, regarding them as the two giants of twentieth century prose-fiction in Ireland. It is too soon for that kind of dictum, for where is the critic equipped to read both Joyce and O Cadhain with equal acumen? Yet the comparison is of some interest. Both men were realists with mythic minds, they were both intoxicated with words, both had a sense of life at once comic and compassionate and saw mankind as forever in exile blundering about in worlds half-realised. I'm not sure whether in fact O Cadhain won't be seen to be *il miglior fabbro*, having learned in the last resort to keep his myth to himself.

3.

These nine stories have been chosen from O Cadhain's earliest books: two ('Son of the Tax-King', and 'The Gnarled and Stony Clods of Townland's Tip') from *Idir Shúgradh agus Dáirïre*, 1939, and the others from *An Braon Broghach*, 1948. Selection of the stories, arrangement, method and style of translation, are my own, with whatever limitations that may entail.

Certain of the minor placenames have been translated, whenever their meaning adds to the feel of the story. Personal names have been left in their Irish form, omitting marks of vowel length as being of no real help to the English reader. Surnames are rare: a person is usually particularised by adding the Christian name of father or mother. Thus, Padraig Choilm is Padraig son of Colm, Tomas Thomaisin is Tomas son of little Tomas. As for the language, I have tried to avoid Anglo-Irish dialects and pseudo-dialects; O Cadhain's language is cool and classic, and free of the self-conscious mannerisms and the melancholy word-music of the Synge-song school.

EOGHAN O TUAIRISC

The Withering Branch

I remember that Sunday night as well as the night just gone. The spacious loft in the Long Barn. The ladder worn smooth. An empty doorframe at the top of it. Creaking boards, and the hole I put my foot through the first night ever I stood in the loft. Planks along the wall stretched on lumps of stone. A miserable bit of a tin lamp hung from a nail. An immense gable at the farther end. Halfdark at the near end where a number of little schoolgirls were gathered chattering like magpies when the music played or someone sang. Bright bursts from the melodeon in the farthest nook. The push amongst the crowd by the doorway whenever a newcomer came to join them from the ladder. Necks stretched, eyes peering in the dim light to see who had arrived . . .

The floor was empty except for Pa the Post dancing with the lady Irish-learner who used always stay for a month at Peait's place this time of year. Then Bill the Schoolmistress's son got up along with the nurse's daughter. Soon Sonai Pheaidi and Liam Mor's daughter the Yank made another couple. At that time I was as keen to dance as a kid goat of a month is to frolic. Though tall for my age and well-built I was only a few months past seventeen, and many there knew I was hardly six months out of short trousers. They all knew I hadn't yet taken a razor to my cheek. And any youth whose short pants are still fresh in public memory, and who is known not to be shaving, had better not be too

13

forward in engaging a woman to dance when there are only three couples out of a full house on the floor.

The 'one-step' was new to this corner of the country, and was still regarded with that distrust which countryfolk always have for the up-to-date. Not until very lately did anyone in the parish undertake to do it, apart from the nurse, the two schoolmistresses, Meaig the Shop, and Nora Mhor Phadraig Neile who had been taught it by the Irish-learners.

I was proud of my skill at the one-step — every bit as skilful as those who were now sailing a zigzag course about the floor. I was possessed of the zeal of an evangelist anxious to publish to one and all, not the truth, but my own talent and daring footwork. For I was on the brink of being a man, though people yet didn't respect me as such.

—A wonder you don't have a go? said my comrade Meaitin Pheadair.

—Indeed I don't know, I said offhand. I was reluctant, being sensitive at that time and having some sense of humour. If a few more couples got up . . . but they weren't stirring.

—Will you take a turn? Mairtin Bhairtlimeid asked Maire Choilm, pretending a gruff voice to hide his impudent daring. Maire was unwilling to refuse Mairtin else she wouldn't have got up, that was evident. Soon Mairtin had to face the gibes reserved for the one who breaks the tabu. A titter went round the wall. It quickly became a hum of mockery and malicious humour. —That's the boy, Mairtin! —Fine tacking. —Keep her in the eye of the wind. —Time now to reef her mainsail. —Whatever else, keep Beltra Rock dead ahead of you!

Mairtin had been a boatman awhile, but he didn't let these squalls put him off course, though he became entangled a few times with Pa the Post and his Learner. But what harm? He had broken the tabu. Reluctance was thrown aside, a couple got up, followed by another couple, and still another. All in the house who could do it were now zigzagging about the floor.

Now I was aching to be out too. But I knew that every

woman who could do it had been swept off already. The
upland women were bunched together in the gable-corner —
down from the mountain pastures, where would they have
learned the one-step? To take out a woman ignorant of the
dance would be the worst thing a youth taking himself to
be a man could do. I thought of the short pants, the shaving,
the malicious humour about the walls a while ago . . .

—Here's Nora Mhor Phadraig Neile coming in, said
Meaitin Pheadair. That's the girl that can do it. Dammit
man, have a go at her.

Meaitin was mocking me, I think, he had no idea I'd
have the nerve to tackle Nora Mhor. But I had, being on
the brink of manhood . . .

However, I failed to engage Nora there and then, for
Liam the Little Hill was just then performing one of his
multifarious duties — chasing out the gaggle of little girls
whose chatter bedevilled the dance-beat.

—Be off! Stand from the door a minute till I chase this
mob of children home. Don't think you'll hide from me,
Neainin Thaidhg! He caught hold of a wild little black-
haired one and bundled her bodily into the group. —Nora
Mhor, don't let Saeirin Johnny slip by there, she's the
ringleader of the bunch. Asleep this rabble of kids should
be. Maybe you'll not be so keen to come here when you're
ripe . . .

I think now, as I thought at the time, that Nora wouldn't
have come to dance with me except that she was flustered
by the officious Liam the Little Hill and didn't get a chance
to see who precisely was asking her. In fact I had her out
on the floor before she had a chance to draw a breath in
the loft.

Not a man there that night but would have butterflies
in his stomach to be dancing with Nora Mhor. Even Pa the
Post who had his Learner in hand, or Sonai Pheadai who
was employed as a beater at Forster's huntinglodge with
scope among the young slips of Protestant servants. But I,
who was on the brink of manhood . . . Nora was a delight-
ful dancer. Tall, well-made, and the way she walked a road
or across an empty floor, this is what earned her the title

of Mhor — Nora the Great. Her body was as light as a living
breath of music as she went weaving in and out through
that dance. Not the slightest imbalance to be felt in her,
unlike other women when dancing. Again and again she
took me through the turn-about as elegantly as a sailingboat
takes its rudder. Tip of my right hand barely touching her
arched shoulderblade. My face but a hair's-breadth from
her cheek, flushed and warm, and her breath quickened by
the exercise making my blood tingle. Aware of the curves
of her breast lifting and drooping to the pulse of the tune . . .

No need to say she was attractive. I knew that already
from the first Sunday night I had ever come to the loft.
But the Lord had never before granted me to come so close
to her person that as well as see her attraction I could feel
it. Her face, I thought, wasn't precisely beautiful. Too
narrow, too sharp for the warm complexion touched on
the cheekbones with crimson. As if the painter of the
Mona Lisa, not softening his first red layer of colour, had
left the face unfinished. But the beauty lay not in her face
but in her eyes, they enhanced features which otherwise
might be said to be skimped. Those eyes could be melting
enough to mollify the passionate rage of a Cuchullain, or
again remote as pools that tantalise a traveller thirsting in
the desert. Her look was usually proud and challenging,
letting it be known she was aware of her own worth and
that none was a match for her. But when she was in the
sulks or in bad humour a flinty glint came in her eye and
even more of a flush into her features, to put one in mind
of Maeve's face on the Plain of Muirtheimhne seeing the
Connachtmen suffer a wholesale slaughter come of her
own implacable whim.

She had such a look in her eye just then. Vexed that I
should have asked her to dance, that she should have
agreed before having a proper chance to refuse. Vexed that
I didn't know precisely who she was. Vexed that I hadn't
given her the opportunity of turning that skygrey look
sharply upon the whole gathering — to show that she had
come in — instead of snatching her into the whirlpool of
the dance as one might do with any common or garden

female there. I would have been frightened by that look in her eye, had she not relented. Yes relented, in fact this woman began to eye me attentively, something she had never done before. A youth not shaving yet, not six months out of shorts and living half-a-parish away, would be unlikely to catch the attention of Nora Mhor Phadraig Neile. But whether in my boy's fancy saving a royal maiden from the gaping jaws of a dragon, or rescuing the Holy Grail from the profane claws of the infidel, I couldn't have spent half the 'fire and energy in either of these exploits as I spent on the one-step in that dimlit loft. Nora must have become aware of my dancing. And I still don't know whether it was in appreciation of my footwork or in pity of my zeal that her eyes suddenly looked into mine. The flint-light faded, her eyes became as two dewdrops sparkling on a roseleaf under the first breath of a virgin sun on a summer morning. That mild look was more killing than the angry one. I was in love with Nora . . .

Who wouldn't be? Any handsome woman at twentyone makes easy conquests. But this gliding seabird of a girl. A match for Cuchullain or Red Hugh. For Nora was no pretty plaything, hers was no gentle, pliant and fernlike beauty, she had rather the style of the mountain ash, taut and elegant, at its best on a bleak edge in the teeth of storm and stress. She might have been Fionnuala McDonald come back again, the Black Princess, Emer, Maeve, or even Redmane of Macha. She would have queened it in Cruachain once or in Emhain Macha . . . The music came to an end, awakening me.

Nora stood negligently by the doorpost. A troupe of young women closed round her as the Pleiades cluster close round their leading star. Easy to see how the women acnowledged their inferiority to that commanding spirit. Just as the sun lights dark planets within its range until they are thought to shine of themselves, so for the young women to be on friendly terms within the orbit of Nora was enough to draw the men's attention to themselves.

From then on she was in brisk demand. Swept off for every dance. Every corner she stood in drew a crowd.

Unthinkingly the women repeated what she said and how she said it. Men went to the top of their flirting fettle with her in word and look. And Nora behaved at her own sweet will, sharp and incisive with this one, mild with that, encouraging here and promising nothing, elsewhere giving a flat refusal. She conceded nothing to any of the men who came within reach. Untouched by their barbed innuendoes, wearing nonchalance like a shield. Pierced them with that rich look. There were men there who would fast a Lent and go through fire, water and wounding steel for the love of that look.

I hadn't the ghost of a chance. But I hadn't yet given her up once and for all. No. A youth during the first fit of manhood is irritable and arrogant enough to stand alone at Watcher's Ford in the teeth of the entire host of the Tain and meet the thrust of his opponent challenging to a duel with flashing blow in face of all the demons out of hell, so long as he feels the faintest hope of getting what he wants. I was in the throes of that onset. The onset of manhood, that's what had irked me into asking her to dance. And she had come out with me! Given me as much encouragement as she had to any man in the house so far. If I could only seduce her enough to let me see her home . . . see her home, only the one night even. I'd be well and truly then among the men. Gone sailing at one clean leap – where instead of a leap those of my own age usually crawl – from the grazed commons of boyhood into the grassy meadow of men. From then on I'd have the perky self-assurance of a champion in my courting, and the fastidious taste of an expert. Unlike the raw youth all wrapped up in the first easy woman he meets when he first goes girling. To see her home would be something to be proud of. Something to tell. 'The hero's slice' in the old tales, which those of my age and kind would go to Watcher's Ford or to the gates of Hell to get.

I know now that love wasn't the only thing to whip me on. Wanting to be a man, wanting to win where scores had failed, to triumph, to be spoken of among people, to give a savour to my name beyond those of the same name and surname — wanting that folk should know of Peadar Choilm Mhairtin who never saw him, never knew his father Colm, his grandfather Mairtin. That desire which has undone so many.

I was a good while watching my chance to approach Nora and take her out dancing again. At last when the night was near an end I snatched at her. It was a one-step, she came merrily enough and had a fair amount to say. Having carefully observed the progress of the hunt during the night I knew she wasn't yet snared. Soon I began to put out feelers and to bring my request to a head as if it was the last thing in my mind. But with Nora it was difficult to keep up a soothering and ambiguous style of talk. Youth is eager and in earnest, disdains the sweet-tongued falsities and the smooth flatteries of age, especially when great things are at stake, an empire to be overthrown or a woman to be seduced, one that might have been a queen in Cruachain or in Eamhain once . . .

—What do you say, Nora, to my seeing you home to-night, if there's no one —

—You . . .

At once she let go of me, there was a dangerous light in her heavenly eyes.

—The cheek of you. A little grabber of a boy.

I'd never have gone at all, I think, to the house-dance at Tom Learai's had Coilin Mhaidhc not been nagging at me all evening to go. The three-mile walk was a penance, for I was bone-weary having spent the week struggling with red kelp. I was more in the humour to go cardplaying as I did on Sunday nights since my bicycle got knocked up. And that's exactly what I'd have done too if I could have changed my mind when we got there, for the unaccustomed walk was telling on me as well as the hot unhealthy air within the house. It was a new slate-roofed house, and the kitchen needed all the space and ventilation it had since almost the whole of the young population this side of the parish had come.

I got a seat by the old couple in the chimneycorner, and

could have all the cigarettes I wanted from a son of Ruaidi Choilm lately home from England, but yet I wasn't at my ease at this dance. It was a month since I had been to a dance in a house, long enough to make me feel out of it, an Oisin returned from the Land of Youth to find not the Fianna but a strange and alien people. I knew them of course, was even intimate with them, they were in fact the very same crowd I met at the Sunday-night dances. The young folk of the half-parish were all here tonight, of all ages from little girls of seven up to myself who was close on thirtytwo. But not one of those who used to be in Stiofain's Loft when I was young and stepping out. Some of those were married, some in America, the remnant never came to a houseparty nowadays. I was myself the last to give up. The most daring and practised dancers here tonight were just about beginning to go to school when Stiofain's Loft was in full swing. As for me, I was still in the one groove. I could still dance as lively a step as ever I did in Stiofain's Loft. Not tonight however. There was some uneasiness niggling at my mind. A kind of barrier between me and the young people enjoying themselves, an invisible frost, it chilled my feelings each time I tried to break through it.

Another swarm came in the door, young girls, grown girls, little girls from school, and a spinster I didn't seem to recognise in the crush.

—Who's the big one? asked a stripling from the Lobster Keys who was near me.

—Hell, d'you not recognise her then? That's Nora Mhor Phadraig Neile of our townland, said Padraig Bhaibin from Tullybrack. —Dammit I thought she'd never cross the threshold again to go to a time. It's three or four years now since she went to a time in her own village. I don't know what got into her to send her the whole way up here tonight.

—The want of a man! Since the men aren't going to her she'll have to go to them. I'm told she's left high and dry.

But I listened to no more of their chatter, for Nora and her party had moved through the crowded kitchen to the opposite corner. It was a long long time since I had laid eyes on her and at once I felt a touch of delight, for it seemed that one slight link with my young days and with Stiofain's Loft remained unbroken. Easy to see she was a stranger here by the ceremonious welcome she got. She was shaken hands with, as none of her party had been, and given a chair in the chimneycorner over beside the woman of the house. It seemed the family had made up their minds — that Nora unlike the others hadn't come to dance and to chance the luck of the night, no question of that now in Nora's case, her dancing done, her chances vanished, a tide that would never fill again.

Soon the girls who had come with her were swept off to dance and sat about afterwards on the men's knees. Apart from some schoolgirls the others, warned perhaps by the spirit of youth in them, kept their distance from Nora: to be on the market is an infectious disease, they mustn't come in contact with it. No one stayed near her except two or three playboys having fun with her to pass the time till they were ready to go for the young ones and the mature fillies. But Nora had wit and a sense of humour, though I noticed she was careful now what she said, unlike the days when her idlest word was repeated like holy writ.

—Wonder you don't ask Nora Mhor out, she wasn't asked yet tonight, remarked Coilin Antaine as he lit a fag-end from Peadairin Rua's cigarette.

—I prefer the young ones. Just my measure. Size fives. I never care to tackle the old maids except when I'd have a drop taken, at a wedding say . . . She's a shade thick in the waist — man, I have to go roadmaking on the Letterbeg bog tomorrow.

—Here, take out Neainin Thaidhg for the half-set, I'll take Saeirin Johnny.

—They'd hardly be too pleased, said Peadairin uncertainly. That pair have been in demand for every dance all night. But anyhow they can only refuse us.

The playboys beside Nora got up too, but it wasn't Nora they asked out. Upon my word, I'd ask her myself!

As I made my way across she bent her head, leaned aside

and began to chat again with the woman of the house. She didn't expect this. I knew by the sudden flush in her cheek she was flustered, in two minds whether she was being asked or not. However she made no objection and came. The dance was a full-set, and while the groups were getting out, placing themselves and waiting for the music to commence, Nora stood by herself on the edge of the set and glanced about the house. She stood in the midst of that gathering, bewildered, as the great horned beast of the Tain surrounded by the hostile raiders after its wild career, yet haughty too as the ghost of Alexander upon the fields of his victories. She shrugged contemptuously, with a quick touch smoothed her piled fair hair, compressed her lips — she was biting off, I felt, what she had on the tip of her tongue to say. But her looks expressed what she left unsaid, especially her sharp glance at the women. I saw for a second the bright defiant glance I had seen in Stiofain's Loft fifteen years before.

—Well, little girls, who are you looking at? Well, Neainin Thaidhg and Saeirin Johnny, why shrink from me? Though fifteen years ahead of you, I am still the most attractive berry on the branch, the one most out of reach. —

> I was remarked upon, one time,
> An Oisin, last of my kind.

Except that I had known her in days gone by, and hadn't seen her for quite some time now, I'd find it hard to believe she was past thirty. Whether it was her bold stance and bitter feeling of the moment that caused it, her body was as taut and trim, her limbs as shapely, and her blond hair even more piled and luxuriant than in her prime. And a flicker of the old all-conquering light in her features still . . .

Her fright receded in the course of the dance, and I became aware that here was no Maeve no Macha come again. That divine impertinence was gone forever from her eyes. I saw too a few grey hairs through that curling cluster. Her face seemed no longer so sharp and narrow, a once too-red complexion had faded to a pale tone, clear and pleasant, it improved her looks. More chaste, more chastened, now more like the face of the real Mona Lisa, as the agonies of a wounded pride had shaped it. And the onward sweeping impulse of her body was defeated too. Though she could still hold her own in a jig with any young woman there, it was easy to see that the wild flame of youth had died in her, the drag of age was at hand.

But I didn't realise how utterly defeated she was until it was our turn to stand aside as the idle couple in the set and we fell into chat. I thought at first that there was still a trace of the old pert independence in her voice, as on the night she had called me a grabber.

And here again tonight I had made free of her. That did it. I was the only man in the house to ask her out: she was aware of that. Of all here present I was the only one to have seen her as a conquering queen: she understood that too, and made no further attempt to keep up her pert detachment. Her voice had none of its old authoritative ring. In the tones of that voice I caught a twinge of ageing, its sharp anxieties ... she had laid aside her pride out of shame and distress.

This woman, who could find love once at the stretch of a finger and with a flicker of her eye could beguile the most stolid heart, was at the end of her tether. Unless she had a gambler's luck she'd be left in the cold. Her force was spent. She had come here tonight in desperation, where she'd not find one to take her even as secondbest.

—Nora Mhor still has one helluva jigstep, remarked Padraig the Pasture's son to a young one sitting on his knee.

Nevertheless she wouldn't find anyone to ask her to dance again. A guttering butt-end, that's not what was wanted here, but new candles, intact, inflammable. That wisdom is instinct in young flesh and blood which old wiseacres fumble for in their philosophy. Let us dare all, experience everything, while there is still zest in the body and the mind desires, tomorrow we shall be in mind and body no more than the grey spent candle-end.

Nora didn't stay long. A neighbouring little girl, a

daughter of Sean Mheait, left her home; the rest of her party were out dancing and had no intention of leaving till the fun finished in the small hours.

And a slice of my life went with Nora. She had left me in a critical state of mind, wavering between youth and age. For there is no such thing as getting on in age, a fair age, middle age, last childishness: there is only the bright and the dark, the laugh and the sorrow, summer and winter, young and old; the pride of vigorous health, the prodigal's zest for exile, the reckless jig that fires the blood, the merry laugh in the dread mouth of danger — or slavish commonsense, the cheerless cheek of the philosopher, disease, the crouch, the coffinclothes . . .

I got up. My party nights were over. Strange that one should cling to the good gone by rather than take what the present offered — to marry, go save one's soul, or write a story . . .

I took the shortcut, came out on the highroad. Caught up with Nora at the mouth of the Pasture byway.

It was easy to leave her home tonight.

—The trunk.

She said the word offhand yet there was a touch of stubbornness in her tone. She hadn't agreed to go to Brightcity with her daughter a week ago last Saturday to buy the trunk, and it irked her like a white frost the way it had been perched up on the ledge of the kitchen dresser, adored like an idol. The children having great play with it, opening it, closing it, looking it all over. She hadn't the heart to vex her daughter this final week, otherwise she would have cleared it off into the room under the bed. But tonight, though the daughter might be of a different mind and anxious to show off that expensive article to the company that had gathered, the mother had followed her own inclination at nightfall and moved the trunk into the room — it might, she said, get damaged or scratched where it was.

It was like a burnt spot or a smallpox scar on the face of life, tonight especially since she seldom had a hearty gathering under her roof. It was useful and wellmade, but that was only a chimaera, a ghost from the Otherworld come to snatch away the first conception of her womb and the spring of her daily life, just when the drinking, the high spirits, the music and merrymaking were in full spate. Seven weeks ago, before the passage-money came, she had been as much on edge awaiting it as Mairin was. That her daughter should be off to America was no surprise to her, no more than the eight sisters of her own whose going was a bitter memory still. She had been schooled by the iron necessities of life to keep a grip on her feelings and throttle her motherlove — as Eve ought to have throttled the serpent of Knowledge. It was the passage-money that had set the heather ablaze again. Flickers of affection, flashes of insight from shut-away feelings, were setting her sense and reason aglow with the knowledge that this going into exile was worse than the spoiling of a church or the wreck of a countryside . . .

But it was destiny, must be attended to. The day was agreed. Patch Thomais was gone for the sidecar. Back in the crowded kitchen the merriment had risen to a frenzy; remnants of the wreck of a people, doomed to extinction at daybreak, bringing their ritual vigil to a hurried night's-end climax of wild debauch . . .

A halfpenny candle stood on a small press by the wall in the bedroom, smeared by a breeze coming by the edge of the paper on a broken windowpane. Depth, magic, mystery of unfathomable seas, reflected by the guttering candleflame in the trunk's brass knobs. It was of pale yellow timber, the mother couldn't at once remember where she had seen that colour before — the face of a corpse after a long wake in sultry weather. And a certain distaste kept her from looking into the trunk, that same tabu which had kept her, though she had often tried, from looking at a corpse in a coffin.

—Have you everything? she asked the daughter keeping her eyes off the dimlit thing. There were all kinds of things in it — a sod of turf, a chip off the hearthstone, tresses of hair, a bunch of shamrock though it was autumn, stockings of homespun, a handful of dulse, items of clothing, papers connected with the voyage across. The daughter took her shoes, coat, hat and dress out of the trunk and laid them on the little press to put on her. During the week she had often laid them out like that but the mother had never encouraged her, and early in the night she had implored her not to put them on till morning.

The mother shut the trunk, threw the bedquilt over it.
—To keep it clean. She had long feared that the daughter

once she was in the American clothes would be estranged from her, alien as the trunk. Mairin was in her stocking feet and naked except for a long white shift which she had been at great pains to fix about herself that evening and which she had no intention of taking off until she had reached the house of a relative on the other side. Seeing her like that was to see a vision, the only one which had remained clearskinned and beautiful in her memory. A vision that gave bodily shape to the dear lost Tree of Life, while it made real the delicate and deceitful skin of the Knowledge-Apple — a mother's first conception, first fruit. She had so many things on the tip of her tongue to say to her, the intimacies, the affectionate things saved up in motherlove, her life-stuff, from the moment she feels the quick seed in her womb until the flush of eternity puts out the twilight of the world.

For a month now she had said many things to the daughter, scraps scattered at long intervals . . . that she couldn't care if all in the house were to go so long as Mairin stayed . . . that the whole house would miss her, herself especially . . . that of all her children she was the one who had given her the least trouble . . . that she was fine about a house. But none of all that said what she wanted to say. She felt like a servingwoman, the necklace she was putting about the young queen's neck had broken, its precious stones scattered here and there in danger of being crushed and broken. She felt as if some hostile force were filtering her speech, hindering her from letting loose the flow of talk that would ease the tight grip on her heart. She was aware she could never hope to express the things in her mind in a letter which she would have to depend on someone else to write, and in a language whose make and meaning were as unhomely to her as the make and meaning of the Ghost from the Fairymound. And a letter was a poor substitute for the living contact of speech, eyes, features. Her flowing imagination, floodtide of her love, would run thin and freeze in a niggardly writing.

She was hardly likely to see her daughter again for a very long time. Mairin would have to repay her passage, then earn the passage of one or two more of the family, as well as send a share home. It could happen that the child in her womb would set eyes on her before she did. That American coat, the graveclothes — how tell one from the other? The 'God speed her' that would be said from now on had for its undermeaning 'God have mercy on her soul'. Children often got those two expressions mixed up. And when the time came that in actual fact would change the 'God speed' into 'God have mercy', it would come without a decent laying-out and a bier to be carried, and with no passionate keen. Even the graveclothes, no mother would have them awhile to shake out the folds of them from time to time as a relief to her anguish, and there would be neither name nor surname on a rough bit of board in the churchyard by the Fiord for generations to come. The voyage — that immensity, cold and sterile — would erase the name from the genealogy of the race. She would go as the wildgeese go.

But while such ideas were as a sour curd in the mother's mind, she wouldn't give in to the thought that she would never see the daughter again. Her sense and reason said no, her love, hope, determination, said yes. And it was these she listened to. Yet even if she were to see her again she knew she'd be utterly unlike the simple country girl, now nineteen years old, with a look pure as morningsun on a hillside in the Promised Land. Her lips would have been embittered by the berries from the Tree of Good and Evil. That dark weasel envy in her heart. Experience, that slimy serpent, writhing in her mind. Temper of cold steel in her countenance. The tone of her voice transformed by the spell of a harsh stepmother. Such were all returned Americans. She must reveal herself to her now, as the mother of the warriors in the cave used to reveal herself to her children when every sallying out in search of food was a matter of life and death. Reveal herself to her while her age and ignorance were still unmocked at, while there was yet no wall of disbelief between her daughter's mind and hers . . .

The money, she thought, was the best way to begin. She took a cloth purse from her bosom, took out what small change the daughter might need in Brightcity, and gave her the purse with the rest. The daughter hung it about her neck and settled it carefully in her breast under her holy scapular.

—Look now child you take good care of it. It's likely you won't need it at all, but if you fail to find work soon it would be too much to be depending on Aunt Nora who has her own children to look after. Keep the rug tucked well round you on the vessel. Make free with no one unless it happens to be someone you know. You'll be safe as soon as you reach Nora's house. Even if you have to take small pay, don't overstrain yourself working . . . You will make a visit home after five years. Well, at least after ten years . . . It can't be but you'll have a few pence put by by then. My . . .

She had kept her spirits nicely up to that. But as soon as she thought to break the crust of speech she couldn't find a word to say but stood stockstill staring at her daughter. Hands fiddling with the folds of her apron. Blushing, tears and smiles painfully together in her cheek. Humps and wrinkles of distress coming in her forehead like keys struggling with a lock. The daughter was almost dressed by now and asked where was the small change she'd need in Brightcity? The mother had been so eager to talk that she had forgotten to get a little purse to put it in. Turning to get it she fell into such confusion she forgot the money in her fist until it fell and scattered about the floor. Her idea had been to wait till her tongue could contrive a proper speech, then to hand over the small change to the daughter as a sacred offering, embrace and kiss her . . . Instead, the sacrifice had been ripped from her hand.

Putting away the little purse the daughter felt an envelope in her pocket. —A tress of your hair, mama, she said. I thought I had put it in the trunk alongwith — the rest. She held the black tress between her and the candle, her blue eyes softened, became childlike. She felt an urge to say something to her mother, she didn't quite know what. Her thoughts went fumbling here and there as a stranger might among the blind holes of a bog on a dark night. The

pair of them would have to be in the one bed, the light
out, and a wand of moonlight through the small window
to charm and set free the tongue. She looked her mother
in the eyes to see if she might find encouragement there,
but she remained unconscious of her mother's seething
emotions, locked within, quite unable to crack the fixed
and rigid mask of her features.

She put on the light and gaudy coat, then the wide-
brimmed hat. Part of the preparations for her attack on
life, she supposed, was to spend a long time fixing and
refixing the set of the hat, though she had no idea which
particular slant she wanted. She didn't realise that the size
and the undulations of the hatbrim added nothing to her
good looks, nor that the yellow shoes, black hat and red
coat made a devil's own trinity in conflict with her fresh
and delicate features. But she was ready: hat, coat, low
shoes on and lady-gloves — not to be taken off again. She
felt strange, surprised as a butterfly that feels for the first
time that it has shed its cramped caterpillar limbs and has
the endless airy spaces unimpeded to sail through on easy
wings. She felt too some of the lightheaded pride of the
butterfly . . .

The mother forgot until the trunk had been locked that
she had forgotten to put a bit of hendirt in it, or somewhere among the daughter's clothing. But she wouldn't for
the world unlock it again. She couldn't bear the daughter
to make fun of her, this morning especially, accuse her of
pishrogues and superstition. She shook a tint of holy water
on her, and while she was putting the feather back in the
bottle the daughter was off out to the kitchen floor to
show off her American ensemble.

The sidecar hadn't come yet. There was a swirl of
dancing. Tom Neile with his back to the closed door was
singing *The Three Sons* in a drunken voice drowning the
music —

> There's many a fine spa-a-rk young and hea-a-rty
> Went over the wa-a-ter and ne-e-e-r return'd.

—Tone yourself down, said the mother to Tom, but she'd have given a deal just then to have a tune like he had in order to release the load of her love in a spilling song. The girls had gathered again about the daughter, scrutinising her rigout, although they had been a week looking at it. They gave the mother no chance of keeping her company. They thought nothing, it seemed to her, of driving a wedge into nature, one almost as inhuman as that driven in by the immense cold sterile sea. The young women were chirruping of America. Chirruping of the life they'd have together soon in South Boston. Typical of a race whose guardian angel was the American trunk, whose guiding star was the exile ship, whose Red Sea was the Atlantic. Bidin Johnny reminded her to ask her cousin to hurry with the passage-money. Judeen Sheain told her on her life not to forget to tell Liam Pheige about the fun there was at the wake of old Cait Thaidhg.

—Take care you don't forget to tell our Sean that we have the Mountain Garth under potatoes again this year, said Sorcha Phaidin. He said when he was going that after him no one would ever again be born to the race that would attempt to sow it, it was such a hardship.

—Tell my boy, Mairin, that it won't be long till I'll be over to him, Nora Phadraig Mhurcha said in a whisper that all the girls heard.

—By cripes it won't be long till I'm knocking sparks out of the paving stones of South Boston myself, said a redhead youth whose tongue had been loosed by the drink.

—God help those that have to stay at home, said old Seamas O Currain.

The whiskey was circling again. —Here now, you ought to take a taste of it, said Peaitsin Shiubhaine who was measuring it out, heeling the glass towards Mairin with a trembling hand. He splashed some of it on her coat. —A mouthful of it will do you no harm. Devil the drop of poteen you're likely to see for the rest of your life. There was an undertone to his voice, he was remembering the five daughters of his own who were 'beyond' — one of them thirtyfive years gone — and he had no hope of ever

seeing them again . . . —I'll drink it myself then. Your
health, Mairin, and God bring you safe to journey's end.

Neither Peaitsin nor anyone else in the gathering thought
to add, —God send you safe home again. Such ignorance
of the proper thing to say sparked off the mother's repressed
anger. —Five years from today you'll see her back home
again, she said tartly.

—God grant it, said Peaitsin and Seainin Thomais Choilm
together.

—And she'll marry a monied man and stay here with us
for good, laughed Citin, Mairin's aunt.

—I'll have little or nothing to show after five years, said
Mairin. But maybe you'd marry me yourself, Seainin,
without a sixpence?

But by this time Seainin had huddled himself back
against the door and was talking like a tornado to let the
mockery of the young girls pass over him.

—At all costs don't pick up an accent, said a young lad,
one of her cousins, —and don't be 'guessing' all round you
like Micilin Eamoinn who spent only two months beyond
and came home across the fields with nothing to show for
his voyage but half a guinea and a new waistcoat.

—Nor asking 'what's that, mamma?' when you see the
pig.

—Anyhow, you'll send me my passage, said Mairead the
next daughter to Mairin, eyes sparkling.

—And mine too, said Norin the next sister.

The mother felt a bleak touch of her own death hearing
the greedy begging voices of the pair. Years of delay were
being heaped on her daughter's return, as shovelfuls of
earth are heaped on a coffin. And the grace of that home-
coming was receding from her — as far as Judgement Day.
At that moment the children she had given birth to were
her greatest enemies.

She set Mairin to drink tea again though she had just
stood up from it. But she wanted to come close to her
again. She must break bread, make a farewell communion,
weave the intimate bond of a farewell supper with her
daughter. She would tell her plain and straight that she

didn't believe this parting meal to be a funeral meal as far
as home was concerned: there would be an Easter to come,
before the Judgement. But they weren't left to themselves.
Her sister Citin with her family of daughters and some of
the other girls pushed up to the table by the wall and in
no time had Mairin engulfed among them.

The daughter had no wish for food. Her face burned:
desire, panic, wonder, an anguish of mind, all showed in
her cheek. Brightcity was the farthest from home she had
ever been, but she had been nurtured on American lore
from infancy. South Boston, Norwood, Butte, Montana,
Minnesota, California, plucked chords in her imagination
more distinctly than did Dublin, Belfast, Wexford, or even
places only a few miles out on the Plain beyond Brightcity.
Life and her ideas of it had been shaped and defined by
the fame of America, the wealth of America, the amuse-
ments of America, the agonised longing to go to America
. . . And though she was lonesome now at leaving home it
was a lonesomeness shot through and through with hope,
delight, wonder. At last she was on the threshold of the
Fairy Palace . . . Tremendous seas, masts and yardarms,
blazing lights, silvertoned streets, dark people whose skin
gleamed like beetles, distorting for her already the outlines
of garth, mountain, rock, fiord. Her mind tonight was
nothing but a ragbag to keep the castoff shreds of memory
in until she might shed them as flotsam as she sailed. She
was so unguarded now that she let herself be led out to
dance on the stone floor, dressed as she was for America.
In any case she couldn't have found it in her heart to refuse
Padraigin Phaidin.

It irked her conscience that she had so long neglected
him. She began to dance in a lackadaisical way, but the
pulse of the music — that music to which they were beholden
even in the fairyplace — excited an impulse in herself, and
soon in her dappled outfit she was like a young alien deer,
fullblooded, with the common young animals of the herd
prancing about her, inciting her to show what she was
made of, what she could do, while the elders sat around in
sage contemplation. The mother was thinking that if she

was ever to see her again the hard experience of life would then be a dead weight on that lust for dancing. In place of that passion of young and eager blood that wedded her limbs to the graceful movement of the stars, the thin and watery stuff of greying age would be keeping her tired bones fixed on earth.

Nevertheless the mother was closely watching, not the daughter, but Padraigin Phaidin who was dancing with her. There and then she guessed the whole story. Easy to see. Very likely the pair had never said a word of love to each other. Very likely they hadn't said a word tonight. And they were likely never to say a word in their lives. But she realised they would be married in South Boston in a year's time, in five years, ten years even . . . She was vexed. That's what lay behind Padraigin's wild dancing fit. What she had failed to say in words he was saying in dance. Body and limbs he was enacting a perfect poem, with growing zest, abandon, vigour and precision, until a lash of his nailed boot carved a spark out of the hearthstone in time with the final beat of the music. Some might put it down to intoxication, but the mother knew better. That spark was in fact a finishing touch, a final fling of the spirit in full victory. Then hardly waiting to be asked while still breathless from the dance he began with easy power to sing. And the mother forgot the daughter listening to him:

> The garden's a desert, dear heart, and lonesome I be,
> No fruit on the bough, no flower on the thorn, no
> leaf,
> No harping is heard and no bird sings in the tree
> Since the love of my heart, white branch, went to
> Cashel O'Neill.

A young spirit trying to crack the shell of a universe that shut it in, so fierce was his song. By now the mother had come to hate him. An evil being, fingering her own proper treasure . . .

Horse's hooves and the clatter of a sidecar were heard

from the cart-track outside. Music and merriment ceased suddenly. Only Seainin Tolan stretched drunk against the shut door still moaning —

> Ora, wora, wora,
> It's on the southern side of New York quay
> That I myself will land —

the only snatch of a song Seainin ever raised.

—Indeed you'd be a nice gift to America! Devil drown and extinguish you, it's a pity it isn't on some quay you are, a useless hulk, instead of here, cried a youth who could stand him no longer.

The trunk was taken from the room and set like a golden calf on the table.

—Take out that and tie it up on the sidecar, said the mother.

—It might get broken, said Mairin. Leave it alone until I'm ready to go out along with it. That trunk was her licence and authority to wear an elegant hat on her head and an ostentatious coat on her back instead of a shawl. Without the trunk her lady-outfit would be an insult to God. If she let it out of her sight for as much as a second as like as not those tricksome and showy garments would wither into rags and ashes about her body.

She turned now to say goodbye to those who hadn't the strength to accompany her as far as the king's highway. Crippled oldtimers who could barely manage to shuffle across the street; for most of them this was likely the last time they'd leave their own firesides for a social occasion. This was the first link of the chain to be jerked apart, it made her feel for the first time how hard the parting was, how merciless. Whatever about the rest of the people, she would never set eyes on these again. In spite of her distress and hurry she looked closely at each one of them so as to store up in her memory their shape and features. She kept a grip on her emotion and broke down only when she came to her grandmother at the hearth. She had as much affection for her grandmother as she had for her mother,

and made more free with her. And was loved in return.
Never a week went by but the old woman had laid aside a
bit of her pension to give her, whatever else might be
behindhand. The old creature was as speechless as if already
turned to clay. In fact she almost was, for the best part of
her was in the grip of 'the One with the thin hard foot',
and the rest waiting on busy death to prepare her dwelling-
place. Her mouth was as dry as the timber of a new-shut
coffin, and except for a faint blinking of the eyelids that
brought her far-off look a little closer to the here and now,
Mairin would have thought that she hadn't the least notion
what was going on.

—I'll never see you again, mammo, she said, her voice
breaking at last in tears.

—God is good, said the mother, a shade stubborn.

Then to kiss the small children and the infant in the
cradle. She felt it as a warm substantial summer after the
midwinter chill. Charming her senses against the threat of
the graveclothes.

The mother brought her off to the room once more.
But they weren't long there till Citin and Mairead came in
on them to get their shawls so as to accompany Mairin to
Brightcity. The mother could have melted them. How
officious they were — without them, she thought, the lump
of sorrow in her throat wouldn't have hardened again.
All she could say to Mairin was that she'd have good
earnings; that she hoped they'd have good weather at sea;
and for the life of her not to forget to have her picture
taken beyond and send it home.

—My own darling girl, she said picking a speck of fluff
from the shoulder of the coat and giving a hurried quirk
to the hatbrim, though the daughter at once reset it her
own way. And having glanced quickly round the house she
was ready to go.

The sidecar went lurching down the rugged village track
followed by a dense crowd, men, women and children.
They had all the appearance of a sacrificial procession: the
sidecar like a funeral pyre ahead, puffs of the men's
tobacco-smoke hanging in the early morning air, and

Mairin walking in her barbaric costume as the officiating druid.

The mother walked alongside the daughter and offered to carry her rug, but Brid Sheamais snatched it and carried it herself. She had determined to have Mairin under her own wing on this last walk, but Citin and her own Mairead thwarted her once more. Then all the young girls closed round her, some chattering and laughing, some so lonesome at her going that they hadn't the heart to say much, and others sorry that they weren't in her place or going along with her. By this time the mother had hardly any feelings of regret left so angry was she with the rabble that wished to deprive her of her daughter before she was even out of sight. She took a spleen against the sidecar too. It was moving as fast as if it was giving a corpse 'the quick trot to the graveyard'. It seemed to her that it was the trunk — perked up on the box of the car, its timber blond as an ear of corn in the rays of the virgin sun — that was pricking the horse to death's own scything speed. She hadn't a word left to say . . .

There was a mild red light from the sun just up. Field walls and piles of stone grinned bleakly. In the little pokes of fields slanting and rugged the tramped stubble was like the head of some Samson having suffered the shears of Delilah. A small sailingboat just out from harbour with a fair wind scratched a bright wake down the Fiord. Mairin looked back from the rise at Hollycliff, from then on her own house and the village houses strung around would be out of sight. Last year's new thatch joined the old black and withered roof at the ridge-strip — line of contact between the past and the time to come. And the village seemed asleep again after its brief second of action, slight as a spit in the ocean that the sailingboat might obliterate.

The sidecar halted at the end of the track. The people formed a close group in the mouth of the highway so that the mother was cut off from the daughter. Just another stray stone in the cairn, that's all she was. The same as if she was neither kith nor kin. More than ever she begrudged Citin and Mairead their going to Brightcity with Mairin.

When the kissing began the women were like a gaggle of
scavengers about a prey. They pushed their way rudely up
to her daughter, squeezed her hand, snatched kisses one
after the other like a flock of starlings on a trash-heap. The
men shook hands with her, shy, laconic, seeming to say it
was all one, and if it had to be done then it were best done
as quickly as might be. Padraigin Phaidin did likewise, but
unlike the rest of the men he gave the slightest lift to his
head and the mother caught the eyes of the couple inter-
locked for the nick of a second.

At last it was her turn. She hadn't kissed her daughter
since she was a child. But she failed to put much yearning
and anguish into the kiss, though her lips hungered for her.
Hadn't she kissed all and everyone? Hadn't all and everyone got ahead of herself in the kissing and hugging? The
daughter's kiss was cold and insipid, the good skimmed
from it by all that had been pecking at her. Her body was
cold too, cold and insubstantial as a changeling from the
Liss.

But what quite spoiled the kiss for her was the sight of
the trunk, she was unable to keep her eyes off it and it was
all but whispering in her ear —

> No mortal kiss will break the spell of the changeling,
> seduced by pleasure to wander and forget, whose
> dwelling is the golden web which young desires weave
> from the sunlight on green hills far off from the here
> and now.

Mairin was now on the sidecar. Mairead sitting beside
her, Citin next to the driver on the other side, Padraigin
Phaidin fixing the trunk firmly between them up on the
box. Damned spirits, they appeared to the mother — the
accursed trunk, Mairead greedy to get her passage-money,
and Padraigin Phaidin on edge to get to America and marry
her daughter — three damned spirits torturing her first-
born and best-beloved.

Padraigin had finished and the people were moving aside
to make way for the horse. The women started in to sob,

and the sobbing lifted into a loud wail of words, expressing no real anguish the mother thought, beyond voice and tears. They wouldn't leave her even the comfort of keening alone. And she shed no tear . . .

She stammered uncertainly, —I'll see you before five years are out. And couldn't raise her eyes to meet the eyes of her daughter, not if the sky fell.

The car was now moving. Sobbing the daughter whimpered, —You will. But now the mother's heart as well as her commonsense knew that she would not. Padraigin Phaidin would see her sooner and the girls of the village and her own children, even the infant then in her womb. The mother realised she was but the first of the nestlings in flight to the land of summer and joy: the wildgoose that would never again come back to its native ledge.

Tabu

Neile went up to the window in the west gable, the airiest window in the new house. There was no one stirring — unlike other Sundays — about the Irish College up at Dromnamona. Nothing to be heard but the shrill cries of the children at ball-play down the garths, and the faint pulse of the tide in the inlet, landlocked, curled serpentine between the two headlands, Rosrua, Rosaileach. She could see the whole way down to the Beak of the Reef. Not a sail the whole length of the narrow fiord winding all the way down to that underwater reef. Nothing but fine-weather sparkles under a brilliant sun, except for a thin fleece of foam on Caitlin's Rock in the narrow channel by the Beak. In spite of herself she let her eyes linger on that treacherous rock-splinter and its little angry swirl. She had always kept from looking at it, since the day twentyone years ago this summer it had drowned her husband and the twelve who were with him on the way home from a pleasure outing to Bereport. A fine summer day like this, it was clear in her memory, disaster came to her out of a blue sky. She was straining the potatoes for the dinner at the time, down at the old house, when she was startled by the rumble of the Fairy wind. The whitethorn at the back of the house shook like an angry serpent spraying poison from its mane. Afterwards she had heard it said that those in the boat were drunk. But long before that, and since, she had heard boatmen say that a fine-weather swirl-wind on the fiords was far more

40

dangerous than the sharpest winter blast. But the harp-string note high in the whitethorn was what lingered most sharp in her memory.

She turned her back on it, that white fringe of foam had left her tied to hardship for twenty years.

She went into every one of the downstairs rooms. She was halfafraid of the spaciousness in this new house. —It wouldn't be so big and empty if it had a suite of furniture, she murmured to herself. Each single room in it seemed as big as the old house itself; and the old house had been made look even smaller by the little huxter shop she had set up in the attempt to make ends meet after her husband's death. But it was the pence scraped together in that old house and in the little shop that had enabled her to have this new house built. For her only son. It would be ready for Sonai and herself to live in within a fortnight. Lucky he had found that job in the parish school. He'd begin teaching in a month's time. She'd be finished slaving with earth and animals, finished with the halfpenny-scraping in the shop . . . Overcome by her feelings she had to come out into the open air.

She went back down the cliff-path. Going through the gap at the back of the old house she shivered in spite of herself. She had scratched against a branch of the white-thorn — it was reaching out as if trying to detach itself from the cliff where it grew, grasping at her she thought, taking her to itself. Here, it appeared, was the cursed spirit which haunted the house whose many generations had been afraid to interfere with it, though it was in the way, and though they had been often badly in need of firewood. If the builders wished to put a gate to the yard of the new house just there they wouldn't be one bit shy of tearing up that old relic of a thorntree by the roots. And Neile wouldn't be the one to stop them clearing her evil genius from the face of the earth . . . Twenty years now, whenever that old thorn made the least rustle her heart had palpitated in fear.

She sat on the step of the haggard opposite the old house door. With the palm of her hand she smoothed back her hair, it was still fair, though a few strands were flecked with grey. She flicked a few specks of dust from the clean check apron she had on over her homespun dress. A pretty butterfly touched her cheek, then at once it was a vicious insect thirsting for her blood. On the slope of the hill above her sunlight and shadow continually fluctuated, changing every couple of seconds the appearance of the scanty potato patches, until light and shade were fused together far up in the ravines of Lettermoyle Hill. Though it was past four o'clock heat-bubbles were still rising on the Bottoms, the great swamp at the base of the hill. Against the light the air was full of dustmotes, she could see a swarm of gnats forming there in the sultry heat of the sun. She watched awhile the tips of sunbeams glinting and sharp on the candles in her shopwindow. Every Sunday about this time she sat like this with her thoughts. Today, unlike other Sundays, her thoughts didn't wander along the wellbeaten tracks of life here in the upland pastures until some young fellow or other came looking for a packet of Player's Weights or a little girl for a bar of toffee. She was aware of a certain change in the light-hearted day, as if everything she saw was being drawn in, being melted and transmuted in the sun's furnace, so that the bright patch was dark, the butterfly a stinging creature, the dustmotes sharp and poisonous insects. She went to walk back up again to the new house, then made a wry face, having to return and serve Maidhcin Pheadair Anna.

Before she went behind the little counter to get the Player's Weights for Maidhcin she went down into the room, smoothed a crease from the tablecloth, straightened a cup on its saucer, came up to the kitchen again, set the pot-oven of mashed potatoes closer to the fire which was half-out, and put fresh embers on the meat-pot.

—You didn't go with the Irish-learners today, Maidhcin?

—No indeed. They were going too early for me. They'll be hard put to it to make harbour on this tide if the calm continues. It'll be sharp tacking the whole way up.

—No sign of them yet is there?

—They were at the Beak of the Reef as I came to the

top of the hill. Of course, Sonai went with them?

—That pair that were with him in the Training College were here at the window waiting for him before daybreak, and they took him off along with them.

—That could be. A sea-trip will do him good after being twelve months cooped up in Dublin above. I suppose he'll be off to Crokepatrick with them next Sunday too?

—He might . . .

—They're coming, merry and gay! said Maidhcin from the doorway. D'you hear that melodeon they have? They should be at Caitlin's Rock any minute now.

She was vexed by the young fellow's talkativeness. She was flustered looking for his halfpenny change between the till and the pocket of her homespun. Perspiring — the sultry heat of the kitchen — she had to rest her elbows on the ledge of the counter, her ear was on a level with the little windowpane.

—You'd think there were whirlwinds out there, said Maidhcin humorously. He grinned at the dust, the withered leaves, the skeletons of last year's vegetation, the wisps of straw from the haggard, all swirling together in the yard with the hum of a winnowing-fan . . .

She handed him the halfpenny. She took the delph, took the cloth, off the room table. Threw the potato-mash into the pigfeed. Put the meat away in the bottom of the dresser. Then she went out again, all feeling drained away, back to the step of the haggard. The whirling stinging storm which had taken shape a short while since in the voracious mouth of the channel had set the inlet for a few minutes wallowing furiously between the yelping confines of the two Heads, and was now spending itself high up in the mountain hollows. The sea had calmed down again, except for the dark wrinkle in the wave foaming on Caitlin's Rock.

Despite herself her eye fixed on the big empty house. Then she went in firmly for the hatchet. From this day forward she'd be free of the thorn tabu.

Son of the Tax-King

This Castle of Clonbeg is a fairly ancient one. The Burkes built it — the loud and arrogant Burkes lusting to possess every sod of ground in Connacht — as they had built scores of similar castles to safeguard their estates and swordlands on the Galway Plain. Estates and swordlands were gone, the Burkes themselves impoverished and dispossessed, no more than peasants and ploughmen on the very lands of which their ancestors had been lords and heirs to whole districts. But the castle still stood. Those massive piles of stone encrusted with moss and lichens seemed to stand of set purpose, corporeal images, reminders of a wrong once done and then again undone.

Among the Burke castles Clonbeg was one of the most dilapidated. It had once been a spacious building, but being long since deserted it had continued to slip and fall until the roof went altogether and the jagged sidewalls were unstable. The violent thunderstorm of some years back had done for the greater part of it. It had knocked the east gable to the ground, the sidewalls unsupported had followed soon after and lay in shattered masses scattered about. It was a wonder to all that the fierce lightningflash which had struck the castle had left even a stone standing, for it had cut a crevice seven yards long out from the castle, making an abysmal hole in a waterlogged hollow towards the south corner of the greensward. But the west gable remained intact — the gable which had its back to the

bleakness of the irrational West, and faced the fertile cul-
tivated Plain — that gable still stood, last of its warlike
phalanx, loath to relinquish its immemorial watch on the
Galway Plain. It was commonly said in the villages round
that it too was cracked and daily splitting apart, yet it was
erect still, an immense stone symbol to be seen for miles.

It had been gapped and bitten into many times. A large
mass had been gashed from its northern edge and more fell
every day. Seen from a distance that gable-edge looked like
nothing more than a gapped scythe-blade or a sawtooth
sickle. The other edge had lasted well, apart from a few
slight dints it was almost untouched. The gable itself was
tightly laced with ivy interspersed with patches of moss
that in this dry weather became dust to the touch. Both
ivy and moss had spread and established themselves with
the years and now hid the entire face of the gable apart
from an odd stony streak still bare. At its base lay a rubble
of stones, powdered lime and mortar, stray chips of oyster-
shell, there a solitary boulder, there a window-lintel which
had been thrown far out on the greensward when the walls
fell. But the gable itself was the most remarkable sight. It
looked like a tough old warrior, hacked and solitary, still
guarding the gap in the teeth of the attack while his kins-
men lay mown down all sides of him.

People seldom made free with this solitary relic. They
agreed to a peaceful co-existence, kept away from it, were
careful to keep their stock from going near it. The castle
precincts had always had a bad name before ever the gable
touched by the thunder had become untrustworthy.

The crows had made their own of this 'bare ruined choir'.
Every year they nested in the chimney and their cawing
was loud and harsh in the ears of anyone working nearby
or having occasion to pass. Though the chimney was choked
where it had crumbled on top and a large slice had fallen
into the chimneyflue, the crows found no fault with it.
It suited them perfectly — here they couldn't be inter-
fered with when settling in, nest-making, hatching. They
could alight up there, haul in their sticks, trash, fur, and
emerge from it on wingflick. At their ease. Daring the

boys of the townland to plunder their nest. Though the boys itched to do so, forever skulking and prowling about the castle, try as they might it would defeat their best efforts to plunder the nests of Clonbeg.

Nevertheless they tried. Tried many a time to climb up inside the chimney, but halfway up the flue was packed tight with stones and mortar-rubble. Outside, whatever chance they might have on the sawtooth northern edge they had no chance at all on the other. But even on the northern edge they made little or no headway. There was one big stone left loose and jutting out, and the boldest and most persistent of them feared to go near it. It was perched precariously on the angle of the gable about eleven feet from the ground, ready to tilt like a plank-bridge, with no chance of crossing it, no chance of gripping it lest it topple and crush the one daring to touch it. The Forbidden Fruit, Taimin Sheamais Sheain called it when he found it moved at his touch. The Forbidden Stone anyhow: misfortune and death for the one who thought to master it.

They tried to take advantage of the ivy on the gableface, but it was so stiff and brittle that it gave unexpectedly and came away in whole sheets from the wall. None ever got higher on the ivy than as far as a thrush's nest a single storey up . . .

They decided it wasn't worth bothering about, one miserable crow's nest, while there were many nests elsewhere still to be plundered and sly destruction to be done on many others of the youngsters of the air — robins, yellowhammers, swallows, not to say cock and henblackbirds and songthrushes.

Off they went, plundered and divided the spoils. But this particular Sunday evening Hanley's son, Seamaisin Pheadair, felt no desire to go plundering elsewhere.

He let the others go and lingered alone on the castle greensward. He hated to leave the crow's nest in that gable, seeing that nests as difficult had been totally wrecked. To leave it there seemed unfair to the yellowhammers, blackbirds, songthrushes, misselthrushes. It was to belittle the schoolhouse crows, and the crows that had nested in Micil Sheain's chimney. Every time he thought of Micil Sheain's chimney his eyes took on a halfscared look, and he blushed for shame. That was the day Mairtin Rua had called him a good-for-nothing — he had lost courage halfway up the gable-end. Of course he had robbed a nest in Oakwood afterwards which was twice as difficult, but that made no difference. His fame as a plunderer had yet to be saved. He eyed the castle long and lingeringly; as he gazed at the crest of the gable the fear in his look changed to desire. He appeared to count every spur and pinnacle, every gap, groove and angle, from the houseleeks fluttering in pride high up on the coping-stone down to the bottom course hid in a heap of rubble. At last he turned, looked all sides as if he feared to be taken by surprise, stole quietly over to a small height by the west ditch and spent another session eyeing the gable from a distance, then went quickly to the south ditch but made no delay there, then scrambled on to a cairn of stones slightly to the east of the wrecked remains and gazed awhile as before. But he remained longest out in the open field sharply scrutinising the saw-tooth edge. From there he went at a snail's pace till he had arrived back in the greensward having made the whole round of the castle. And made it once more. But on each round he stayed longest in the open field at the back considering the sawtooth edge. Finally he made straight for it, there was a smiling glint in his eye.

He looked about him. This was his only chance to attempt it privately. He'd never do it if there was anyone present. He pulled up his short pants and left his cap on a boulder so that there might be nothing to hinder him. He had no trouble till he came to the foothold below the jutting stone. He could now lay his hand on the 'Forbidden Fruit' and shake it a little. It moved, he saw now that it was barely balanced on the wall-angle, it wouldn't take much to bring it down. Sprung from the mortar, it was altogether loose, if it fell it would crush his bones. But to make any headway up it would have to be crossed, and anyhow it would be cowardly to give up at the first attempt.

He'd simply have to get by that awkward obstacle. Just above it there were two plinths projecting, one on either side – once the lintels of shot-windows or sentry-slits, the uprights on the outside had long since fallen leaving a shapeless hole. But the plinths were still firmly embedded in the gable-edge and wouldn't give. Easy grip them too if one could reach that far. That was the crux. Try as he might, straining himself and stretching his hands, the tips of his midfingers wouldn't come within a yard of them. Pity he hadn't a companion to give him a leg up. But he'd have to go it alone. He'd have to make a clean leap and grip the plinths, else give up. He looked back down at the ground, even if he failed, he thought, and was left on the broad of his back below, what harm – he wasn't so high up, and there was a bright green patch of sward right in at the butt of the gable where he'd fall.

He tensed, stretched his arms and jumped into the air. The leap left him empty. He felt his thighs tingle from the effort, seemed to have knocked his forearm, dangled from the two plinths like a long string from a spiderweb. But he'd soon be a ghost if he stayed that way. Already the small of his back was aching. He drew his knees up inch by inch till they touched his chest. He was reluctant to swing his body and hurl it in on the loose block of stone, it would be a fearful thing to let go his grip above in a leap. But leap he did. Bruised a kneecap hurtling on to the rough surface of the block. It seesawed under him, he gripped the gable-edge till it might stop moving, and till the pain had subsided. That pain was agonising, he could barely keep back the tears that welled up in his eyes. Terrified in every limb – the swaying stone, it would slide from under him and take him tumbling down along with it. But he found the grit to endure, the pain receded, the stone swayed less, though it increased again whenever he made the slightest movement. At long last he took courage to stand up on his feet and examine what he could see of the rest of the wall above. Emboldened by the thought that, since God had granted him to overcome that stone-block hostile and challenging, it'd be a hard case if he couldn't make it the rest of the way. He studied the gaps and nooks, the projections, the bleak and jagged spurs above him: from the ground they had looked grim, they weren't nearly so bad from close up. He grew almost dizzy when his eye caught the cap-stone far above. But again he nerved himself against disaster, clenched his teeth, tried to count the stones and nooks that would give him finger and foot-hold. He couldn't be certain for some of them he couldn't see very well, afraid to stretch his neck in case of losing balance and falling headlong. But now his climbing path was clear, it was rugged and difficult, yet it could be done and done more easily than the part of the way he had come.

Again he set to. At times the going was easy, at times he went at a snail's pace. But he drove himself on, clambering over jags, stretching across fissures, huddling through hollows, going astride projections, until he reached a sharp incline which had a wide step at the base of it. Here he could rest and examine the next stretch. At this point the thick mane of ivy which covered the gable-face was somewhat sparse. A brief glance through the ivy-strands was enough to tell him that that face of the gable was split, the split was too high to be seen from the ground and concealed by the ivy. Looking closer he saw it was an immense crack, coming right through the wall, making two halves of it from top to bottom, or nearly so. Cracked by the thunder, he thought, a few years ago when the lightning struck. He realised now that this gable too had been split . . .

It occurred to him that the crack might be handier to climb than the gable-edge. He inched across towards it, daring and careful. He had to be for he was now on a plank-bridge in earnest, on a narrow projecting course of masonry across the face of the gable. When he reached the edge of the crack he saw he had been right — this was the best way to attack the wall. The wall was split wide-open, great chunks of the rubble had fallen but the cut stones were still in position flanking the rims of the crack. It would be no great hardship, except for the obstructing ivy, to clamber along the cut stones up the gable. Standing spreadlegged on two of them, and always gripping one above, he began the ascent. It was strain and struggle, ivystalks thick and tenacious were always ready to trip him. At long last he was able to embrace the coping stone at the peak of the gable and there, as they say, an end. He raised a knee on to the stone, drew up the other beside it, and went crawling and hunkering to the inner edge and let his legs hang down in the gap between the coping and the chimneyflue.

Exhausted as he had never been before. Breathless and wheezing. Drops of sweat formed in the cleft of his forehead, dribbled down stinging his cheeks, ran quick into each other slicing along his jaws and neck. Ears full of the hum of his heart beating, lips flecked with foam. And worst of all he was paralysed in every limb.

He let his head sink on his chest and rested. In time his heart quietened, the numbness went, he came to himself again. But he kept his head lowered, eyes closed, afraid to look down, he might become dizzy. He would have remained a long time like that but he was startled suddenly. Frightened by a hoarse complaining squawk. A crow flickered up out of the flue and skimmed flappingly by. There he found himself, perched as high as a sailor aloft on a masthead. The smooth Plain was spread out all round him, yellow rays of sunset softening the green of the young corn and sending golden darts through lit hawthorns fencing fields. His eye lingered on oak groves on hillsides, leafy hedgerows along winding lanes from which dense clouds of dust arose, and trim little villages in limewhite clusters on the expanse of the Plain. A flock of sheep were moving towards a hole in the wall, cattle grazed greedily out in the open pasture now that the heat was gone from the day and the frenzy ebbed in wasp and gadfly. Far off he heard the lusty braying of an ass stung to madness by a natural craving. A lone thrush still thrust exuberant song into the wide vault of air, but his song was gradually going off, it ceased at last in a thicket on the edge of a damp bottom half a mile to the south. Then all the elemental world gave way to the trance of sleep. Nothing under the sun's arch broke the drowsy charm except that one querulous crow that swooped and wheeled in the air above its nest.

But where was the nest, and how many eggs — he had never thought of that. No eggs at all in it maybe, after all the trouble it had put him to. Maybe the crows were only making it — but that was unlikely, all crows would be hatching this time of year. Anyhow seeing would settle it.

He moved crouching to the brink of the narrow chimney, knelt and looked down the flue. There was the nest, about a yard down, as cosy and trim a nest as ever was — and a little ring of eggs in the hollow of it like a nutbunch. He bent and reached down, touched and counted the speckled eggs, they were warm from the hatching. He counted them again to make sure — three. He handled them, examined them, turned them up and turned them over, replaced them, and then began to examine the nest. This was the first time he had ever consciously considered a nest. But having gone to such pains for this one he must get all its details exact. Downy fur, moss, feathers, sticks, all cleverly and neatly woven together. The crows must have been at great work gathering all these makings and hauling them to the chimneytop. To watch a solitary crow carrying off a twig or a shred of moss one would never think of the hardship, the great load to be gathered, the uncertainty. It seemed a shame to destroy so much earnest work of beaks and claws. But need he destroy it? Hadn't he the eggs? Just then the crow skimmed the gable-peak and cawed piteously enough to pierce a stone heart. God, it would be as bad to touch the eggs as touch the nest. Wasn't it for the sake of the eggs the crows had struggled so hard? And he'd deny them their comfort! He heard the hen-crow squawking plaintively close by. In fear for her nest and eggs. Yet it was those eggs she lamented which had dragged him too into suffering and danger of death. No matter, the nest must not be robbed.

But since no one as far as he knew had seen him, who would believe he had gone to the top of the castle unless he had some sign to show? If he was to tell Paidi Mhaire or Mairtin Rua or any of the lads in school tomorrow that he had scrupled to plunder the nest he'd be a laughingstock to them forever. They wouldn't credit for a moment that he had mastered the 'Forbidden Fruit' and got to the gable-top unless he had something to show for it. A bunch of ivy perhaps? But every wall in the district was covered with ivy. And there wasn't a block nor even a small stone he might manage to pull out and take away, except for one sharp splinter projecting from under the coping stone, but the like could be found anywhere in the village without lifting a leg from the ground. He thought of the houseleeks which grew thick on the ridge of the gable. But there was hardly a shed roof in the district without houseleeks while, he felt, the only crow's eggs in the country were in the chimneytop of Clonbeg Castle.

No use. Though he was resolved never again while he lived to plunder a nest, to make a close study of birds' nests and their ways, and take a strong stand against plunderers, he must have proof first that he was prince of plunderers, that no plunderer had ever done such a daring deed as get to the top of this castle. Without proof his words would go unheeded like chaff in the wind. No use. He'd have to do robbery now. But the least possible damage. The nest wouldn't miss one egg, and that egg would be enough to tell the world that he wasn't bragging about nothing. And if old tales were to be believed, wasn't that one egg due as tithe or tax, or in some way to be sacrificed? Wasn't it from the tax-egg that the birth had sprung which went on to gather the rent of the whole world in the story — 'Son of the Tax-King'?

That recalled something else to him. After showing the egg to the nest-robbers he would preserve it. Bring it home. Put it under the hen his mother had hatching a clutch of eggs in the coop. Do it secretly, not to be discovered till a chick came out of it — a crow-chick. How he would cherish it, tame it and keep it in, but give it plenty to eat — a perfect bodily proof of the daring deed he had done. It'd have the wild nature and the roosting nature in one. Son of the Tax-King. Who knows, one day it might have rule and rent over all the youngsters of the air.

He went through the eggs again, chose one, nursed it gently in his palm. Son of the Tax-King — conceived within that speckled shell, he would have to mind it like a treasure on the difficult dangerous journey back to earth. They'd see, he'd bring that egg safe to the ground no matter what.

Now he must make his way down. He didn't wish to leave the peak without leaving some clear sign there. He was bareheaded — but anyhow a cap could hardly be seen up there. If he left his jacket they'd knock daylights out of him at home. A pencil in his pocket, useless. Luckily he came on his handkerchief, clean and white, the one his mother had to buy him last winter because the schoolmistress used to make a rigorous round each day thrashing any boy without one, but she had given it up now since none of the lads had a snot to wipe since the fine weather came in, and anyhow he'd have a chance to get one before the wet-nose season came in again. The mistress wouldn't notice it gone, and there was no fear they'd miss it at home.

He pressed the handkerchief against the outside edge of the coping stone, it needed a weight along the length of it else the first blast of the St John's Eve storm would sweep it away. The sharp splinter jutting out under the coping stone would do nicely, just heavy enough, if what was buried in the wall was as big as the edge projecting. Anyhow he couldn't see another suitable stone possible to pull out. But it wasn't as easy as he had imagined to pull the splinter loose. He lay along the coping stone with his chest over the edge and braced his feet against the chimneytop brim, reached one hand down — the Son of the Tax-King in the other — and took a fierce grip of the splinter. It didn't give easily, though it was right under the stone at the crack in the upper course and slanting out. The course had a strong hold on it. He tore away a tough sheaf of ivy which grew luxuriantly under it and pulled again. The whole course above it appeared to shake, including the coping stone on which he lay, but thinking it was his own dizziness due to looking down he let go his grip and shrank back crouching for a spell. He fixed his gaze on the ground below and the base of the gable in order to settle his reeling senses. For the first time he considered the stiff and rugged scramble down which lay before him, having the Son of the Tax-King in his fist as a further hindrance. Still it would be much less difficult since he had discovered the crack in the gable. All he had to do was to be careful of himself and of the tax-egg, taking every advantage of the cut blocks gaping from either edge of the crack and go tacking from one to the other down along. He'd have to get going. Determined to affix the handkerchief to the gable-peak he took a grip on himself, bent again to the splinter, tugged with all his might. Good, it gave, came sluggishly with him — a big hunk, sharp at the base, just the thing. As if he hadn't enough to contend with just then the crow came wheeling rapidly and squawking loud and angry enough to fright the very devil.

But it wasn't the harsh and piercing caw of the crow that sent the splinter falling from his hand. This time there was no mistake, this was no dizziness, the coping stone swayed and moved under him. The whole building swayed, twisted rigid like a straw rope ready to give. That tall bleak gable that had withstood the wars, wild winds and weatherings of the centuries, shook now and trembled with a dull roar from peak to base. The deathrattle of a mighty giant. No wonder. Shaken by lightning, that splinter pulled had unlocked its last grip on life. The old masonry strained and stretched, slow, stiff, as something in the throes of death. Then came again upright — last kick of life. The crack widened in the heart of it. The walls parted on either side of it, reluctantly it seemed, still parted, dividing clean and entire from top to base, then toppled with two resounding crunches heard for miles around. Last remnant of Burke destruction was at last destroyed.

Before anyone could reach the scene the agonising crow had alighted on quick wing and taken to herself the relic of her shattered nest — Son of the Tax-King — which had fallen unhurt unbroken from the dead fist of the boy far out on the greensward where his broken body had been thrown alongside the Castle coping-stone.

The Road to Brightcity

The cock crowing awakened Brid. She yawned and turned over, stretched and settled her head back again on the pillow. But her husband was awake too and shook her.

—The cock has crowed for the third time, he said. You'd better get up.

She was loath to leave the warm soft blankets, but having stretched her limbs again and rubbed the sleep from her eyes she jumped out. She had her new bodycoat on, the candle lit, and was raking live coals from the ashes before her husband arrived on the hearth.

—A wonder you bothered to get up, she said. You'd be time enough.

He made no answer awhile, went fumbling at the dresser.

—A right mess I made of it, he said, taking the little clock and shaking it close to his ear. —I was fully intent on winding it, still and all I went to sleep and forgot it. It's stopped at ten past two.

—May the deathrattle take it. It's four o'clock now.

—If not more.

—I'll have to be off as soon as I'm ready.

—You'd be time enough at five, leaving yourself four hours for the road. I'll slip down to Tomas's place and if young Taimin isn't up I'll wake him. He'd be great company for you, since neither Peige Sheamais nor any of the other village women is going to Brightcity.

—Taimin won't stir a foot for the next two hours most

likely, since he happens to have a customer for the turf. I'll be home along with him if —

—If you don't get someone else.

—What I was going to say was, said Brid using the same wrangling tone as her husband, —if it should happen I'm ready to come home before he is and get the chance of another cart.

—A cart from the Currach. You seem to be sweet on the Currach people.

—I still know them better than I do the people of this village, she said serenely. I'm not five years here yet.

The husband was sorry to have given her that dig, small as it was.

—It's a nasty journey to Brightcity, for the little it's worth.

—What's worrying me is that it won't even be worth that much presently. In spite of all my care three of the hens stopped laying this week, and the fawn cow won't have what'll do the tea shortly. I'm afraid I won't have enough to churn again for a week — even in a fortnight's time I'll be hard put to it.

—A rest might do you no harm, he said, obviously not wishing to spell out what he meant. —You are worn out going to Brightcity one Saturday after another. It's a crucifying journey, since you can't take a jauntingcar like Maire Sheamais.

—It's crucifying enough. But there's no loss on me yet, she said offhand.

He was sorry for her, still he wasn't too pleased with her words. A strong active woman not yet past thirty! Not the way the women who had come before her used to speak. His own mother when she was a servantgirl with Liam Cathail used to go twice a day to the city with a tankard of milk, and no car to give her a lift home. Or his grandmother — she used be home from Brightcity before milking time with a hundredweight of meal on her back and with only two stops for a rest. But the women nowadays had only to go draw water from the well to be crippled with rheumatism the day after.

—I'll be alright if that woman in the Lawn laneway lets me alone, she said, deliberately disregarding his silence. —Only for that I wouldn't be in nearly so much of a hurry — trying to get there before everyone else. It would hinder me on the way to market and it would be late evening when I got home.

—Don't be in any hurry home till you have the chance of a good lift. I'll see to the house.

—Like you saw to it last Saturday — the children would have been scalded by the kettle only Neil Sheamais came in. Unless you want the skin off your ears don't stir from the house till Neil comes. She said she'd be up about ten and won't need to go home till after dinner. I'll have to buy her some sort of a present for Christmas if God sends the pence. Haven't you sally rods to sharpen? Don't bother about anything else. Don't leave a pot where it's liable to topple anywhere about the house. And if Citin cries give her a sup of lukewarm milk in the bottle.

—I will, said the husband drily.

—And send the dash down to Peadar's with Neil, take care would you forget, she'll be churning today. And shift the calf from Glen Garth up to the Height — but for your life don't leave the house, not if prosperity were to knock at the door, without leaving someone to mind the children.

—I won't, he said, a shade stubborn.

—And I'll have to get ready immediately, she said gulping the last of her tea.

—Don't forget to bring a bite to eat.

—Devil a bite I'd need if the woman in Lawn Lane wouldn't delay me. She took me into the kitchen this day last week and gave me a cup of tea. Fine tea. Golden brown. A very kindly woman and not trying to get the better of a body like the rest of them. Her husband is a sergeant of Peelers. She's from Longford.

—I left a creel of turf at a Peeler's house along that road before I sold the horse. She was enticing me to have tea but I didn't go in. I hadn't enough English to deal with her.

—A palefaced woman and not very tall, was she?

—Devil the know I know now. Nearly four years ago.

He swallowed his tea and went out to the dooryard.

—There's still an hour of moonlight, he said when he came in. —I know by the stars of the Cluster that it's not a second past four o'clock. I imagine it'll be a fine morning, though the sky is rather overcast. Nobody seems to be going to Brightcity.

—Only the turfmen. The rest have exhausted their means. Don't you know it's the Dry of the Hens?

—I'll come to the head of the road with you. Or as far as Taimin Thomais till I wake him.

—Fine and early you're impatient to be out! You'd leave the house would you, not knowing — God between us and harm — what might happen the children?

—They're snoring. I won't be two ticks outside —

—Go back in there and sleep for another three hours. I'll be alright.

She went back into the room. The two children were in the small bed snoring softly, and the mother didn't disturb them except to shake a drop of holy water round the bed and sign the Cross on herself with it.

She lifted the strap of the butter-creel, prepared the night before, about her neck. The man settled her shawl over the top of the creel behind and she went out the door.

A rugged and dirty path led from the house to the village road. Water squelched under the soles of her boots and her left foot was already damp before she reached the firm cart-track. She was surprised that none of the village houses showed a light, she had thought that with the steady south wind there had been people would be up and out to snatch red kelp from the beach. Maire Sheainin showed no light either, but she'd be time enough up in another couple of hours since she could afford to take a jaunt on a sidecar.

No matter how often Brid had gone that way on the same errand at the end of night, she was always struck by the strangeness of the sleeping village. That cluster of houses wasn't nearly so bad on a blackdark night. Tonight there were shafts of moonlight sliced between the houses and byres and frightening straggles of shadow out from gable-ends. Needles of moonlight in the grain of the granite rocks glittered cold and hostile, snake's eyes, lying in wait. And the reign of the Moon that would have been so bright and blessed if it hadn't been distorted, was cast now as it were into a phantasma by the hosts of the Otherworld before their silent vanishing come cockcrow.

In that village which would be astir with sound and bustle in three or four hours' time, Tomas's housedog was now the only living voice. Nature's herald warning in a dark tongue that the Master — and his mistress Night — were still locked in sleep and not to be wakened. In a lull of the wind his angry bark rang back from the houses and the walled fields; the sound leaped over into the stony patches, thence to the craggy fens at the top of the townland, it went echoing birdlike from cliff to cliff, rockface to rockface extended it, until at last it died in a querulous whimper on the bare moorlands of the farthest heights.

A stream of shadow from Tomas's carthouse cut across the track. Brid glancing sideways saw the two forked sticks supporting the shafts of the cart loaded with turf, though there still wasn't a breath of smoke from the house. Of course she hadn't forgotten her husband's vexation when she wouldn't wait for Tomas's Taimin. As well as being a neighbour Taimin was also her husband's first cousin once removed. And if she was to wear out her tongue telling him, it still wouldn't stick in his mind that she didn't avoid Taimin from a sense of superiority, taking the chance of a lift home every Saturday on some cart from the Currach — her own village — five miles off on the other side of the parish. That of course was another sort of pride. Though she was five years married now she still felt all the village people to be strangers. She wasn't properly used to them, very likely she'd never get used to them, very likely she wasn't forthcoming enough to make free of people. Anyhow she had no wish for the company of Taimin Thomais. He had been at her matchmaking. She recalled clearly his flaring eyes as he gripped her fingers drinking her health. From that on she couldn't stand the look in his eye. He seemed to her always to have two looks in his eye, a dead-ash glaze, and behind it a flicker of passionate greed and rascality. She couldn't chat with Taimin Thomais without feeling glints of that hidden flame all the time aimed at her. She found it hard to explain, but she knew she felt as if there were sparks burning on her skin when he looked at her.

When she emerged from the village road on to the highway she stood for a moment listening. Nowhere the sound of cart or footstep. A bit early she thought. Else someone would be stirring. Still she had better get along, there were nine Irish miles before her to Brightcity, and better be early than late in getting there.

The moon had declined in the west above the Isles and long strands of her light touched millions of drops of quicksilver across the bay making, it might be, a bridge for the Fairy host to Little Aran. But brilliant as the moon was she had rather a look of melancholy in the empty sky, displaying all her trinkets to dramatise the weight of her despair. Brid longed for her setting. She would much rather be shawled in dark. She could make more free with the dark. By moonlight more than by the light of day a body might easily forget the eternal weft of one's being and think oneself part of the transient material world all round. Brid was happier in the dark, it gave her mind a chance to come to grips with life instead of having the brilliant extent of the view to distract her with thoughts of life's merciless hardship. She seldom had a chance to think, what with pressure of work, children peevishly demanding, or people in. Furthermore, she felt like shirking this journey today. Since she had to go she might as well go at her own pace and not in step with someone else. She could never bring herself to tell her husband that she wasn't so robust, nor anywhere near it, since having that last stillborn child, and lately the long walk was telling on her. And near Brightcity, if she was on her own, she would have a good chance of getting a lift from someone she knew and be saved the worst two or three miles of the journey.

If she was as far on to the east as the wood of Moyle, she thought, or close to it, before the sidecars began to overtake her, she'd have a good chance of a free ride the rest of the way, for by then the drivers would be so near the city that they wouldn't be on the lookout for further customers. But scarcely any driver would take up two, and if he did take one of a pair, which was unlikely, it would hardly be her. And to have a walking-companion taken up would leave her worse off than ever, having been within an inch of a lift. She was always worn out a mile or two farther from journey's end than she used to be, these days.

Wasn't it well for the women with small change enough to spend a few shillings on a jaunt. Maire Sheainin, for instance, up on a sidecar every single Saturday. But she musn't compare herself with Maire Sheainin who was coining money since the war came, and constantly getting handfuls from America as well. She herself had been at pains to spare every halfpenny last Saturday in order to lay a shilling for a jaunt halfway today, but the shilling went where all the other shillings had gone — into the till at the shop.

But if she wasn't clean out of luck she'd surely get a lift near journey's end. Her own neighbour, Mairtin Mor, who never had but the same three, would take her up. Didn't he take her up the Halowe'en Saturday? Or Sean Choilm. Of course if he had four he'd hardly be in the humour to put one more up on the box. Always mumbling about not liking to overstrain the horse. Anyway Peaid Neachtain wouldn't leave her on the road, he was in the habit of coming to play cards since the visiting season started. Coil Liam was the best on the road for a jaunt. She wasn't exactly in love with Mike the Shop — it was a great favour to get credit from him without expecting a jaunt as well. Sure enough, he usually had no more than himself and the brother's wife, apart from those he'd take up along the way, but he'd only take up a good pay, or else someone whose custom he was trying to attract away from the other shop. And Micil Pheige always passed her by. At one time he had been generous with a lift. None more generous. But something had got into him lately. He was infatuated with some crowd he called Sinn Feiners and anybody who wasn't a Sinn Feiner had no longer any hope of a lift. Brid often tried to puzzle out what sort of folk these Sinn Feiners were. Padraig Thomais Thaidhg was in them and had been taken up last year when there had been some kind of a skirmish up in Dublin and on the Plain. But the Earl, as he was called, got him out again. The Earl could save a man from the scaffold, though the Sinn Feiners were loud in their agitation against him. It was rumoured they were drilling with hurley sticks by night and were all set to make war on England. They had a meeting in Ballindrine lately and were at daggers drawn with the priest of that parish. But such doings were no affair of the poor. How should they have any inkling of them? The poor as always had to struggle on.

She went through the one-street town. Though there was light in one or two of the publichouses there wasn't a sinner to be seen apart from two policemen with their backs against the door of Geraghty's Yard, motionless. On the lookout for turfcarts without lights, maybe, though usually they didn't bother with them. Or maybe snooping on the publichouses? What were they talking of, thinking of? What would policemen have to think or talk about since they hadn't the hardship of strand, garth or bog, living in plenty and drawing their pay? Going by the Dunes she heard the noise of a car coming down the track from Ballydonagh, and she was undecided whether to wait for it or not. She had to face the hill of Ardfert. She saw from her by the light of the moon the slabs and pillarstones in the marshy ground on both sides of the road. Like heroes, half-risen, wakened by trumpet sound. —'Often the trumpet spoke, as often was the bloody work prolonged,' if old tales were true. But the woman who had to go to Brightcity often in the tailend of night, alone, at times unwillingly, must put ghostly things and fairy things out of her mind. Brid used to be afraid of these things at first, but she had mastered the fear and become so used to taking them lightly that her only reaction now was to quicken her step a little till she had cleared the hill of Ardfert.

But in that outlandish place there was nothing worse

than Liam the Tailor and some young fellow she didn't know along with him. She recognised Liam's voice at once. She knew — the whole countryside knew — that he used often rip the silence of the night after drinking in the village. As soon as she recognised the voice she slowed up and stood stockstill. But there was no car to be heard, no one on foot, not even the car she had heard a while ago. She owed the tailor money, the price of the homespun suit he had made last year for her husband, and she had promised so often and failed to pay that she wouldn't for the world wish to overtake him now. But the pair were only strolling, and it was still a mile and a half to their own byroad. She greeted them.

—By the Lord, said Liam impudently to the fellow along with him, —when I was your age I'd not let my chance slip so easily. A fine young woman . . .

—I'm bespoke already, she said trying to laugh it off.

Liam let out a drunken guffaw. —Leave it to the Currach, he said, and started in on a long spiel about the quick wit of the Currach folk. Brid judged it best now to be making her way. She knew they weren't dangerous. In such cases she knew a woman was no more likely to be attacked and robbed than plundered in another way. But she was unwilling to linger and talk, especially since she'd be ashamed to mention the money again to the tailor. Yet she found it hard to dismiss him from her thoughts. A coincidence, to have met him of all people. —I wonder is he already telling his comrade about the money I owe him? But he wasn't that sort. Easy to deal with and kept his mind to himself. However, the drink was a peculiar thing. Well she'd have to pay him by Christmas no matter what. But what use was her pitiful few shillings to him? He had a good income without them, if he didn't leave every penny in the public-house and his wife and children at home pinching and scraping. It was a curious world.

She was fine and warm now having walked above two miles. It would do her no harm to take off her boots and carry them on her arm. One boot was letting the wet in, and grazing her foot a little. She threw the shawl back off her head on to the creel and walked more free. She was rightly into her stride now. The blood coursed through her veins like organ music. She didn't feel the road slipping by under her bare feet, the quick walk pleased her, a challenge to life.

After she passed the Leitir byroad there was light in every one of the few houses along the way, and turfcarts going the road. Sometimes five or six of them in a line and the drivers walking ahead in a group together. An odd one with the driver sitting on the spur of the front-board. Many women on the road too, with creels and baskets, in groups, in couples. Others walking among the turf-drivers. Brid knew most of them by sight only. Some of them were utter strangers come for the most part from places well to the east of the village, while she herself had been reared five miles west of it. She had never spoken much to them either, for up till today she had always had her own neighbours along with her. But the companionship of the road is free. Still she simply passed the time of day to each of them without getting involved in conversation. Not that she felt reluctant to talk, but she feared that some of them would be so eager to hold the 'stranger' in chat that she'd fail to get rid of them. It was the fashion for the groups to split up in pairs after the first stretch of the road, and whatever pleasure she'd take in the chatter of a group she was in no mood for a dialogue. The road being so long she was the less inclined for company. Nine miles she thought was a long way, too long to be caught in the ramifications of gossip.

Afraid too that a dialogue would become too intimate. There were dark ideas slinking at the edge of her mind, and bitterness to sting her feelings, but to her conscious mind the drag and drudgery of life never seemed anything to grumble at. Even Mike the Shop — it never occurred to her that he should be complained of and penalised for putting three different prices on the one article according to whether a body was badly in need of credit, or a safe bet, or able to pay on the dot. She was far from realising that man, not Providence, was answerable for the sea of troubles which confined her to struggle and skimp, sent her tramping every Saturday to Brightcity barefoot, left her worrying always, slaving all the time . . . She regretted that such things must be, part of the load to be carried in this Valley of Tears — tragic legacy of the Forbidden Fruit. But it never occurred to her that they might be a personal cause of complaint, no more than it might occur to her as an injustice that she rather than someone else had to put up with foul weather, misfortune, death, or the nightly absence of the sun. Though she understood the ideas 'luck', 'bad luck', 'misfortune', well enough, she was unable to give any precise sense to the notions of 'pleasure', 'joy of life'. But she knew she was far from being easy in her mind, far indeed. What she would most like to complain of was that her peace of mind was shadowed by the unrelenting pressure of external life, dulling the daylight, so that her irritations of spirit were trying to break out in spurts of bitterness . . . Now she couldn't go visit her own people on account of the two children, and the odd time anyone of them came to her, her inquisitive husband and prying neighbours put a private chat out of the question. She'd give a lot sometimes to be able to make free with some female acquaintance, though she knew well that chattering with the neighbours was no cure for her vexation of soul. Give them an inch, she knew, and they'd take an ell. They'd add a sequel to your story as if they weren't interested in hearing it or taking it in properly. Yet she knew it would be a great relief to her feelings to voice her complaint. And she'd prefer to do that with a stranger, someone from far-off, who would attend to it no more than to the sough of the wind, rather than an acquaintance who would treat it as an excuse to launch at length into her own story of her own hardships in plaintive detail, and as an item of gossip afterwards with the next door.

Today it was no comfort to her, as it had often been, to see there were many on the road as hard put to it as she. There were so many dark edges to her thoughts today she feared she mightn't be able to restrain herself if once she began complaining. Her ulcerated spirit was ready to break in bursts of bitterness. She was afraid she'd weep . . .

Easy enough pass out the ones she overtook. But there was a woman at the Ionnarba byroad and although Brid didn't even know her by sight it took her all her time to get out of her clutches. Having only a light basket the woman had no trouble keeping up with her. Brid had to quicken her step so that the woman would have to ask why the hurry and she could say she had to be in Brightcity for a customer who wanted the butter for breakfast at eight. Afterwards she more or less regretted leaving the woman behind, she seemed the kind that sought the company of a stranger, just like herself other Saturdays . . .

Gleneany. Ardnakill. Kylenahalla. The foaming stream at Sruthan. They floated towards her slowly as green-grass places to a traveller thirsting in the desert. She rested at Horsegap. And again on the Quarry Stone a little farther along. She had never felt so spent so soon. She had a sudden fear — 'the fool's run soon finished' — if she dropped exhausted maybe after the first spurt? She'd die of shame if she had to be taking a rest at every turn when daylight came. What would they say? A fine lump of a young woman. And only two children yet. And what about women with twelve in family who were blithely making the journey?

She rested again. The strap of the basket was chafing her shoulder a little, for she had been drawing red kelp on her back during the week. But the moon had set, it was now the thick dark of the night's end. She'd do nicely, hardly anyone now would recognise her if she hurried past. Then she thought of bunching her nap skirt up about her thighs, it gave ease to her legs, they were streaming with sweat. It wasn't the decent thing for her to do — a young mother — she was glad it wouldn't be remarked on in the dark.

But soon again she was desperately struggling with herself trying to do without a rest till she'd have reached the top of the next rise. And she knew she'd soon be rambling in her mind again when she began guessing how many footsteps it was to the next rise after. She faced every slope up, slope down, every turn and twist of the road, with a child's cheeky impudence towards the stern looks of a father. Every foot of the way was a saga surpassing the feat of Watcher's Ford, the loyal boys of Ventry, Goll's patient suffering on the Rock, the black passion of sorrowful Deirdre. Brid, and many another Brid, felt each mile as a Via Dolorosa, each step a Gethsemene, each stone an Apple of Knowledge to be payed for in sweat, worry, hardship and humility . . .

At last she rested at the little bridge of Stonemasons. This was the halfway mark. Four Irish miles to go yet. She wondered how long she had been on the road. Bad luck to that tricksome clock. How long till daylight? But already the morning-star was rich in the east, losing its flush, clear now as wellwater, and a few early birds were astir.

She had never felt so spent at the halfway. Her body was hot from hard walking. Her feet were getting in each other's way and refusing to go forward. Every time she stopped to rest, her perspiring body shivered in the cold. And she felt her legs trembling, above the knees mostly, and stabbing pains deep down in her stomach. She was well aware what caused the pains . . . Heavy loads didn't suit her lately.

She attacked the road once more. Glad of the dark. Her shield. If she were to collapse the best thing to do would be to roll herself into the ditch by the grassy road-verge where she wouldn't be seen till morning. She thought of Neili Mhairtin found dead like that by the hedge at the butt of the Grove. It was said at the inquest that she had been two hours dead before she was discovered. The doctors stated that she died of hunger. One pitchblack morning with pelting rain, and the body found in a nook under the hedge. Still it was strange that none out of the scores that had gone by during that time had noticed her. And left a litter of children all of an age.

If that, God between us and harm, was to happen to herself wouldn't the house be in a queer fix. What would the two children do? If her man was put to the pin of his collar to manage them the one day of the week she was from home, how on earth could he cope with a seven-day week? Eibhlin near scalded herself with boiling water last Saturday though he had promised before she left that he wouldn't stir out to go pottering round till little Neili Sheamais came to take charge. Would he be on the same capering gadabout today? Might as well be talking to the wall. Were they awake yet and starting to cry? Often at it at the crack of dawn. And would he think to put a drop of warm milk in Citin's sucking-bottle in place of the milk gone cold overnight . . .

She took a certain lively satisfaction in thinking how completely her man would fail to manage the children if she herself were to go. But he'd marry again. The children would have a stepmother. She'd neglect them, thrash them if they were cranky or got into mischief. She could expect nothing else from a stepmother, seeing how hard she found it herself by times to keep a hand off them. Children were a great hardship. The agony of giving birth. Two of her own stillborn. That's what robbed her of her young girl's shape, left her with the lazy bones of middle-age. Never the same since. Would she have another dead baby? God forbid. It would be the death of her. Yet welcome be the will of God. Suppose she never had any children at all? Would her man and herself be so intimate then? Or would the children's loud complainings be replaced by a cold surly silence of their own? Would he think it worth while to get up a morning like this to bid her goodbye on the road, if there were no children and he had no reason to say — doubtfully, like today — that he hoped he'd be able to manage them while she was away? She had only to look at Nora Anna and her husband. The pair of them like the lugs of a new tongs knocking no spark from each other, only a dull dead sound. Nothing for the couple to share but a carking solitude, if what was said was true. Brid didn't have carking and solitude to contend with, only the two cranky children.

Cranky. Always cranky or fool-acting. Kept her awake

half the time. To make matters worse the whoopingcough and measles were going and the schools were closed. Misfortune seldom passed her door. If they were to get the whoopingcough or measles it'd be six long months before they'd have shaken it off, which would be no help to herself ... Would she be able to give them schooling? She'd have to, they were due for America. They were saying on all sides that America would be opened up again if only the War was over. They'd have to shift for themselves since she had no dowry to marry them near home with. Hard to keep the older ones to school once they were able to give a hand at home, still they'd have to get a share of it even if it doubled her own work ... Would they be quick in sending money home? Or would they be like her own sister who had promised to send her a bit in her fist three times a year and after the first year never sent a red halfpenny — unless she were to write this Christmas. A couple of pounds would be a great boon. There was good money to be got for everything, if one was in the way, but at the same time everything a body had to buy was four prices. Pigs fetched the best money, but just now her pigs were knocking against each other with the staggers. She wondered whether they might thrive on their own leavings ...

This was Brid always, worrying all the time about the future, attending more to the trouble that might come than to the trouble here and now. It would be a great loss to them if anything happened the pigs. She was taking the bite out of her own mouth to fatten them for the big Christmas Fair in a month's time. They'd be fine and plump by then if she succeeded ... She had a heavy bill at the shop, her shawl was threadbare, her boots letting in, grocery money to pay, tailor's money, manure money. On top of it all the cows were going dry and the hens ceasing to lay. In spite of her best efforts scraping and pinching to keep food in their mouths she'd soon have nothing to bring to the city. From now on the week's supply would have to do for a fortnight.

But these misfortunes were nothing, they were there, could be dealt with. They had shape and body, could be fought. People had wrestled with far more terrible misfortunes for hundreds of years. They would be fought with flesh and blood, with drudgery, careful management, and hope. But new twists threatening to come into the world, a new age, which had yet made no impact on the old traditions of this patient race, that was the prime cause of her unease. No telling what shape they'd take, how they'd appear, how severe they'd be. Life hung in the balance, no telling what might be. She heard old people say it was the end of the world. That the prophecy had come true — this was the 'War of the Two Strangers'. There was great talk of 'Conscription'. If her husband was to be taken from her and killed? So far everyone in that countryside who had gone to the War had been killed. And she was certain, if there was only one single shot to be fired, it was her own man would be struck. They were dogged by that kind of bad luck . . .

And times were becoming troubled even in Ireland. She heard there had been some sort of a commotion over beyond the other day. And it was becoming hard to get food even for money down. It was rumoured that no more tea would come in, flour, tobacco, nor even the brown sugar, and that the soldiers would seize the stock and crops next year if the War lasted.

In that case how long would she have to keep on going to the city? A year, two years, five years . . . twenty years . . . Till the eldest girl was fit to replace her. She herself would be middleaged by then and still more dependent on the journey. Would the look of her face then and the set of her body reveal to one and all her stonewall spirit, hard and defiant? Her back humped from the creel, her feet worn smooth and serviceable taking the long measured strides of a horse? Or walking at a fierce gait. Jawbone bleak as the beak of a currach. Leathery cheeks printed with crowfoot marks like the marks of a milestone. Eyes with a glint of pure steel. Such were the middleaged women she knew, their girls' features beaten ironhard by the weekly managing, the slaughtering Saturday walk.

And would her own children sup this sorrow? If they

could find somebody to send them their passage-money
from America they'd be well away. But like everything
else, who could tell whether America would ever be opened
up again. And for them to scrape a dowry together by
their own drudgery, enough to get them husbands near
home, that was the worst that could happen to them. Then
they too would have the week's contriving to face and the
Saturday walk. Yet who could tell? The world might have
changed by then. In the beginning even the wealthy were
without sidecars, but country boss-men had them now and
the wealthy were tearing about in motors. Who knows, the
day might come when countrymen too would have motors,
just like the Earl. Only lately the bicycles began but some
of the men had them already and an odd woman too. No
matter. Bicycles weren't for married women in the country.
But in this world it was wiser to say nothing. Who knows,
by the time her own daughter was of age perhaps every
woman would have a bicycle . . . But what good was a
bicycle? No way a woman could carry a full creel or a
basket on it, though she had seen messengerboys in Brightcity riding with even more awkward loads. But that was
alright for short distances. A motor, that would be the best
thing for a butterwoman. But she'd not see it in her own
time. Nor very likely would her daughter see it. Nor her
son's wife.

Her son's wife — that son yet unborn — would she be
good to Brid? Would she bring her little dainties from
town and her breakfast in bed? Or abuse her like Una
Caitlin's daughter-in-law? She'd be nice enough, perhaps,
till children came and were cranky. If her son were to
marry, care and children and crankiness would start all
over again — but then it would be the young woman's
business. Still, it would be there, and she'd have to take her
own share of it. But it would be a great standby to be getting
the odd American pound from the rest of her children, and
as well as that the old man and herself wouldn't make over
the land and house entirely to the son until they themselves
were getting the pension. She'd be independent again then.
If she was displeased she could do what she liked with her

money. There'd be a new generation in the house wrestling with the same things which she was wrestling with now. And no more than that to worry her, since she wouldn't herself have the responsibility. She'd have a chance to visit and chat. Spend long sessions in a neighbour's house. But in time she'd be unable to leave the house — or the bed maybe. She knew she'd be reluctant to have done with life. Death would come nonetheless ... but she went no farther with that idea. Spite of the lively satisfaction she had in complaining and thinking of what she had to endure, she saw the 'final fields' far more clearly than she did the cursed crooked ways of life in the here and now ...

Forge Hill. She stopped to rest. She had felt neither the way nor the weariness while she was thinking. But she was fairly crippled and ached with the hunger. She began to eat her lunch, glad now she had brought it. Seldom had she been so hungry before reaching the outskirts of the city or thereabouts. The dark was thinning out, a grey sky whitening in the east, but there was a heavy mist, a touch of rain in the wind. She had a sudden fear the day might turn out wet, if it did she'd be wet to the skin before she got to Brightcity. What harm but she had to go to the market. Her clothes would dry on her skin and she was sure to get the devil of a dose. Still she wasn't quite so worried as she had been. She'd have as much of the road put by before daylight as on any previous Saturday. She was hardly a mile from the village of Moyle and that's where the side-cars overtook her always. But she'd have to get beyond it for if they had a seat to spare they'd still, as far as that village, be on the lookout for a woman with money. The slice of dry bread refreshed her, but she was taken with a hiccough, gulping in her throat as the tide's suck sounds in a hollow of rock by the shore.

   She forgot the hiccough as she passed the byroad to Badgers' Peak, for she began to think of Larry the Peak. Dammit her father should have given her to Larry when he came asking — it would have shortened her road to Bright-city by about six miles. And she wouldn't have half the slavery. Or if she had married Paid Concannon from Derrypark, she'd be within call of the city with nothing to do but get up fairly early, milk the cows, sit up on her ass-and-cart and take the milk into town. But bad luck to him he was too old. Anyhow she wouldn't be keen on going in and out of the city twice a day — not once a week if she could help it. Pity she didn't go to America when she got the chance instead of giving in to the old folk at home.

A long loud roaring. Ship Rock. A sign of filthy weather, a woman from there told her one morning they walked together. A squall of wind whistled through the chinks in the loose-stone walls and screeched sharp and hoarse in the telegraph wires. She set herself silently to say the words of a song — Padraig Choilm's, *I am up since the moon was rising this night gone by*. But she had no more than two verses. Then she began on a story, 'The Knight of the Black Laugh', her uncle's story, Micil Mhairin, to cheer her bleak and lonesome state of mind. 'Hot it was and heavy. Hard they made the soft earth, soft the hard, till they caused the ground to tremble the length of nine furrows and nine ridges away, and forced wells of spring-water up through the grey rock with the dint of their conflict.' She took pleasure in the reverberation of the words in the nooks of her memory. But she hadn't that story either. Strange she couldn't pick up things like that, for at school she hadn't been too bad. She must buy a newspaper today if she had a penny left over after laying by the price of a pint for the carter who would carry her home. She'd read it for her husband tomorrow and tell him how the War was shaping. But she doubted whether she would still be able to read it, it was so long since she had taken up a book or a paper. At least she'd be able to spell out the price of pigs, that's all he'd want.

When she reached the peak of Leana Hill the houses of Moyle appeared to her in strange distorted shapes through the foggy gloom. She was never too fond of going alone through that village by night, though she had done it once or twice. It had a reputation for robbery since the old days, though she hadn't heard of anyone being molested there for ages. Moyle had now been for two generations contrite and behaving well, but that wasn't enough to clear its name. Anyhow even if there were highwaymen there in hundreds it wasn't her sort they'd go for. The houses strung together and hung up above the roadway like a flock of eagles ready at any moment to swoop on their prey, that's what used to frighten her, and that was all.

The flow of her ideas was suddenly halted. There was someone in front of her on the road. A woman, a basket-woman. She had been so wrapped in her thoughts that this woman took her by surprise. She had come a long stretch of the road since she had last seen a human being. It was Peigin Nora from the village next her own, and she stood in the middle of the road waiting for her. No chance of shaking her off, a rabbit would more easily shake off a weasel. She felt helpless. Having avoided company all morning she had company now whether she liked it or not. And to think that the sidecars would be along any minute now. Peigin Nora of all women. All the women disliked her she was so loquacious. And disliked specially by the jaunting-car drivers. She often took a jaunt and quiffled the driver out of his fare. At least that's what Brid had been told. She was in a right fix now, no car would take up two, even if one of them wasn't Peigin Nora.

Against her will she listened while Peigin talked like the clappers of a mill. Grinding all sorts. The price of things. Price of transport. Conscription on the way. A big American liner sunk, laden with Christmas moneyletters, as well as tea and tobacco. The staggers and whoopingcough in the village at home since yesterday. And fever again in Letter-geeha. Mike the Shop to give no more credit to certain people unless they cleared their accounts this Christmas. A daughter of Tom Beg's coming home — it wasn't exactly known yet who the man was, but the priest tomorrow would be scarifying . . .

Passing the premises of Mairead the Pub Peigin asked her in, a halfglass of whiskey each would warm their hearts. But Brid knew she couldn't afford to call for a second round, and anyhow she never took a drop herself apart from an odd fingerwidth at a wedding or christening. Though she was inclined to think that a halfglass of punch would cheer her up if she had the price of it. She told Peigin to go in on her own, she'd wait for her. But Peigin wouldn't. She regretted having done Peigin out of her consolation, for she was well known to be fond of a drop. They tramped on in step together. Peigin now hadn't so much to say. Brid's thoughts were free to scamper like wild things through her mind. Her feet above all, nagging at her more than ever, would the last three miles knock her out altogether, she'd have to put on her boots again coming close to town, the worry was would they blister her feet on the last stretch. Getting wetter too, no wind, and a filthy drizzle fit to bedraggle and drench a body unawares. Looking back to see if there was a sidecar coming, only then did it occur to her to let down her bunched-up skirts, though she had intended to do it before reaching Moyle. Dark was fading bit by bit, daylight becoming distinct between her and the shawl of mist over Moyle Wood. Not a sough of wind in the wood today, silent and still as the breath of death under the bare trees, big wet drops fell from their tops in dirty splashes, angry 'bad luck' spits.

In Wood Valley farther on they were overtaken by the first of the sidecars — three one after another. Two of the drivers didn't even glance at them. Mairtin Mor in the middle one had looked as if he could hardly believe his eyes that there were two of them, studied them as if to resolve them into one to fit into the one empty seat he had up on the box behind him, winked at Brid towards the empty seat, and finally after some consideration shook the reins and set the horse to a trot up the rise. Next minute Coil Liam passed them with only two up. Brid knew he'd stand her a lift only for his intense loathing of her companion. Maire Sheainin was on this car. She barely nodded to Brid who'd swear she had a smile in her eye when it was clear Coil Liam had no intention of taking her up. Further along Micil Mor took up Peigin. Micil was the best in Ireland for a lift, and he'd prefer to take up Brid but, conscientious, thought the older woman more in need of it. —You are fine and strong and young enough for the road, he said. I'd take you if I could.

She came at length to the fork in the road. She knew if she took the road to the left she had a poor chance of a lift, nearly all the jauntingcars went to the right where there were more houses and they could make better headway. She lingered a good while in two minds about taking the righthand road, but the cup of tea she had got the week before, having gone to the left, banished every other idea. Nothing so refreshing as a cup of tea like that after a journey, it'd warm a person up wonderfully to start the day, instead of having to wait till one or two o'clock after doing the market and shops and then to be hardly able to drink it with hunger and weariness.

She hadn't gone far up the slope when she heard an ass-and-cart trundling behind her making a great effort. A cart from that district on the edge of the city, loaded with a variety of foodstuffs — potatoes, cabbage, root crops, a basket, a tankard of milk. A lone woman perched on the front shaft feet dangling and with every clout of the reins on the ass's rump drove him up the slope. Brid was on the point of asking her for a lift, but the woman had too much to attend to, hadn't time for a word or even a glance.

She met another ass's cart of the same locality, coming from the city having delivered the morning's milk, no need to spur the ass, he was trotting nicely of his own accord. A woman sat on an upturned empty milkcan, a longlimbed fullbreasted woman, obviously wellfed, bordering on forty. Brid didn't even know her by sight, but she thought at once of Paid Concannon's wife, the one he married when his offer for herself had been refused . . . Another sidecar coming. She was sorely tempted to look round, but was ashamed to. It was Sean Choilm, she recognised his growling 'hup' even before he came up with her. He'd certainly take her up, he had four passengers, but he'd hardly think it hardship on the horse to put another up on the box for the short bit of road left. But he passed her out without a word or a look . . . She was surprised to see him coming this lefthand road. But he had Cait Cheaite up, and she remembered telling Cait where the woman lived who had held her up last week. Cait was smart enough for anything.

She hadn't quite reached the top of the long rise when she heard another sidecar coming at an easy trot. She looked round in spite of herself and her heart jerked. Paid Neachtain. Many a time he had warmed himself well by her fireside since the cardplay season began, though she hadn't seen him for almost a fortnight. And he had only three up. It was hardly worth her while to take a lift now, only an Irish mile or so to go to Boherbwee. Still it was worth it, that mile was the worst, the hill was so long and monotonous. The horse was almost up with her, slackening on the slope. Paid merely shook the reins, flicked the horse setting it at full stretch passing Brid at a gallop up the hill. She nearly dropped where she stood, she wouldn't have believed it if she hadn't seen it with her own eyes. Now she wouldn't have wished for a fortune that she had looked back . . .

She trudged on uphill. She had to pull the shawl up over her head again, the thin mist was penetrating. Though the fog had lifted it was black and threatening to windward, it would likely come pelting any minute. She'd be saturated before she had her business done, bought her parcels and things and be ready for a cup of tea in the eatinghouse. And then maybe left to linger in her damp clothes until she'd find a carter to give her a lift home.

At long last she got to the top of the hill at College Wood within the suburbs, big commodious houses at hand, the first fringe of streets only a little farther on, Boherbwee but a quarter of a mile away. And nothing left but a downward slope to the city boundary. She set down the creel in a nook of a tall hedge. She'd have to put on her boots. Tying the laces she thought again of the cup of tea she'd get if the Peeler's wife delayed her. Somebody else might have got there ahead of her. Hardly likely. Pity she ever told Cait Cheaite. The world's best wheedler that same Cait. She'd try it anyway, the very first thing, though it'd bring her a good bit out of her way with maybe nothing but blisters to show for it. No use in delaying.

She slipped the cloth off the load in the little creel to make sure all was trim. There lay the pat of butter as innocent and pretty as Little Rushcoat when the Mettlesome Hero woke her from sleep. A waterdrop in the printmark and the butter fine and firm, unlike the mess summer butter makes. She unwrapped the eggs from the straw and paper and counted them again, yes, three score, scoured clean and pure, white, brown, pale blue. In no particular order, yet she knew the egg of each and every hen — the little grey pullet's, the speckled hen's one white with hardly the breath of a shell, and those of the crested hen brown and big as duckeggs, she was fond of those and would have liked to boil an odd one for herself since the Dry of the Hens came on only she didn't care to do it in secret. Strange poor creatures hens, God love them. But only for the care they got they'd have long ago died out. She wrapped up the eggs again and tidied the straw about them, drew the cloth over them and was ready to go once more . . .

The drizzle was over now and the air clean. Southeast, the sun. Scallopping with light the edge of a mass of raincloud, dark and threatening, breaking bright through it and beautiful, making the wet leaves in the wood and the raindrops on the road twinkle like jewels. As if the sun were rising upon the brink of victory, having endured and overcome the burden, the dangers, the disgrace and hardship of the night. Brid looked back along the road. Back along those nine crooked miles with which she had grimly struggled. She realised she must do them again, again and again. Do them till her jawbones showed bleak, her limbs weathered, the hard look came in her eyes. But she had them done for today and that was something. Her pulse throbbed, her heart sang. She was gamesome and happy, knowing the pure high-spirits of a young wild creature, and her body was as a scythe with a new edge to it eager for the swathe. She was ready again to take up her share of the burden of life. She gripped the strap of the buttercreel . . .

The Gnarled and Stony
Clods of Townland's Tip

1.

He lived up there on the gnarled and stony clods at the top
end of the townland — Ballyanny, townland of the swamp,
on the bog's edge, in which even the best bit of land would
have been nothing to boast of if bone strength hadn't been
spent in cultivating the red moorland these twentyfive
years past, and the rock conquered by the generous sweat
of youth. Old Peaits had seen the moorland being broken
and bearing the following year a crop fit to bring the flush
of health into the wasted cheek of an invalid. He saw the
rock conquered and a team of horses ploughing where the
foxes had made their dens. He had seen the farmers on the
Plain below him giving away their Irish for a crackle of
broken English. And to bring it home to him, some of the
young men of Ballyanny were sporting hard collars and
silk ties.

But the gnarled and stony clods of townland's tip had
neither been broken nor conquered. His own holding was
the same as it had been a quarter of a century ago — a strip
of red bog, a strip of rock, and an odd patch here and there
fit to nurture a crop. But if the holding was unchanged it
wasn't so with Peaits. For some time now he was a much-
changed man. The youngest among the townland people
thought he had never been any different, in mood and
manner, from what they had seen since they sprang up.

The older generation thought that, along with the normal oddity of old age, he had become glum, taciturn, begrudging, from never having married and from living on his own in that lonesome secluded little cabin up at the far end of the townland. The young folk were inclined to make fun of him from time to time; one can hardly blame them, nor blame Peaits if he turned the mockery back on themselves. Those who had come to the last lap of their lives – his own contemporaries, though he was the oldest of them – understood best what a great change had come over him. They had seen his fluent exuberance failing, and the merry spirit of dissipation that goes with it. They had seen him in the first lap of his life, hearty, fond of a joke, a great rambler. At his peak they had seen him eloquent, generous, philosophical. And they saw him now hard and inhospitable as the immense wasteland at his doorstep. His mind had shrunk into itself, he had shut himself off from everyone, especially from the young. And though at times he was still nicknamed Peaits the Songs, Peaits the Stories, Peaits the Folklore, none of the young folk, none even of those who were well on in life, had ever heard from his lips a song or a story if they wanted one.

Actually it was nothing bad-natured in Peaits that caused his taciturnity and his boorishness, that had quenched his exuberance, fossilised the story in his heart, locked the song under his tooth. No, rather it was the unbearable burden of having to spend what was left of his days among a generation of people who were alien to him and his traditional style. He understood in the depths of his old and lucid love that he was the last and late survivor of his people; understood that his lore, his tales – he had hundreds of them – had been valued. Valued! Yes, valued of old by a people to whom they were the first morsel at the feast of life, and that now they were considered rubbish by the latest line of young people whose only attribute was an elegant pretence of English ways and speech. He knew he was no longer wanted. He would never again dress out a story handsomely or turn a stave of a song for the rest of his days . . .

He who had learned *Erris Flannan* from the mouth of Sweeney himself fifty years ago at a patron-day in Connemara. He who had been in the alehouse down the County the day Raftery had composed *Mairin Stanton*, having wagered a quart for it with the alewife. He who himself could shape a ditty or construct a verse of a song when the mood came on him, in that vital time gone by when people were goodnatured, when a man might get a day and a night's lodging for a tale or a new song brought into a backward corner of the country . . .

Now neither old nor young had need of his lore. The impudent upstarts of today had no more regard for him than for — 'the chaff of barley lifted on the wind'. And alone in his small hideout in the presence of the fire of turf and pinelogs, in the half-light of his outback cabin at townland's tip, out of his passion he could recite nothing but the verse:

> The young folk can't fathom me
> So full they be of English pride
> Neither can they fathom themselves —
> There's some sense in my rhyme.

The years slipped by. The last spark of the Fenian plans and preparations was extinguished. The Land War lost its character. But neither Fenians nor Land War had scratched as far as the gnarled and stony clods of townland's tip. And as for the lone man up there, the crust of age and taciturnity closed him off more and more from men and from mankind.

2.

The townland was agog. No one knew who he was, the stranger who had come to visit Peaits on the gnarled and stony clods of townland's tip. A proper gentleman, he came in a carriage, he had spent four consecutive hours with him there in the cabin. What brought him? And he came again and again and not a sinner to know what he was up to. A lawyer, come about a will, some said. He was a distant relation of Peaits, born in America, took a trip to Ireland, no worldly limit to his wealth, said others. In fact some of the old women went so far as to say that Peaits had discovered a treasure, that he had a small pot of gold in the house, and that he was being advised by this gentleman concerning it. No one thought of that other treasure, the wealth of tradition and tune. Naturally they didn't think of it for the nicknames 'Peaits the Stories', 'Peaits the Songs', were long forgotten. No one imagined that the Irish might still have a sap of life in it, that a Gaelic League had been set afoot in Dublin, that a man named 'Nice Little Branch' was beating pathways through the Plain unearthing lore and sources, and gathering the songs and stray verse of 'blind' Raftery.

The day came when Peaits was seen spruced up and taking to the road — in a direction which the youngest to the best of their recollection had never seen him take. And even the gander who had the nerve to come into conflict with him at the Marshpond at the edge of the village was made to understand that it was no go, and that even an upstart gander had better behave himself in a most mannerly fashion in the presence of old people 'of a travelling kind with a mind for action', who carried moreover a fine knobbly length of a blackthorn stick.

3.

I the most skilful in string-sweetness
Never my equal will be found.

Three weeks from the day he departed, Peaits was singing and satirising again in Nuala Tim's alehouse on his way home to the gnarled and stony clods of townland's tip. The old glum heart was merry again, the scowling bitterness of not being valued and the crust of taciturnity quite rubbed away. His journey had been fortunate. At the great literary gathering, the Oireachtas, he had taken the All-Ireland Award. He had been the most exact in song and story, the wittiest in ditty, the most authoritative in lore, in all the four quarters of Ireland. He had outclassed all the oldtimers of the land. After the Oireachtas he had been detained in Dublin for a fortnight, to be lionised, to have an anthology gathered from him, to have his songs and stories put in writing so that they might be there for the Irish people to read as long as grass grows and water runs. Now he was on his way home, a little drunk, small blame to him.

—What do I care what they do, the upstarts of the Anny? he was saying to the alewife, calling for another jug. —How long before they'll get the respect I got? How long before a gentleman in a coach and pair comes to another door in the Anny asking a single creature of them up to Dublin? . . . They have small regard for me — alien greenhorns — but I received honour where the most well-to-do, the swankiest and most anglified among them wouldn't cause the turn of an eye. They hold me in contempt . . . but I'll give them to understand on my way home who are the aristocracy, who are the upstarts, who are the fickle seed in the land . . . where the old stock is . . . and whose is the natural talent and intellect. Another jug, alewoman . . .

And though the alewife tried to impress on Peaits that he should go careful on the drink, since he was unused to it during the years he had shunned company, it was all to no effect. He drank and drank, sparked up a song, spilled folklore, and abused the people of the Anny in the tavern far into the night . . .

Actually poor Peaits was being unjust to the Anny-dwellers. Since he went they had heard and read what honour he had earned for the townland, and they regretted that hitherto they hadn't better respect for him. And to make up for their former neglect they tidied up his little potato-patch and saw that no harm came to his old milch-cow which was the whole of his stock. If it was known in the Anny when he was due to arrive no doubt they would have lit a bonfire and made merry with him till morning.

The world had turned the corner of the night when Peaits arrived. And not unmarked. Not seen, but heard. He began his litanies at the Marshpond. He recited aloud their genealogical branches and the ramifications of their kindred up through the village. Not a soul was left unscathed. Everybody's ears were red as a result of that night.

And old Peaits himself did not come safe. He had his own mishap. He lay stiff at the cabin door when the cattle were being driven out next morning. And old Nelly Fahy told me that it was Dublin unmade him, that it was unseemly for him to have gone there at all, that the long journey had afflicted him, that the unaccustomed drink had put his heart to flight . . .

And since old Peaits' cabin fell some years back there is no house now on the gnarled and stony clods of townland's tip.

The Hare-Lip

Nora Liam Bhid spent the night as she had spent the previous one making tea for the wedding party. But now the light of an early February morning, fogged and white, was seeping into the halfdeserted parlour, and since she had cleared up after yesterday and was now free, again the strangeness of it came nagging at her. The strangeness of being married, the change, the outlandish Plain: that same flicker of unease astir in her ever since the night her father came home from the Galway Fair and began telling her mother in private that he had 'fixed up a strong farmer on the Plain for Nora'. And it had been no cure for that cut-off feeling to see the man himself and his sisters for the first time last week at the matchmaking. Like a female salmon locked in a choked up sidechannel and destined never to reach the breeding beds in the clear shallows upriver. Nora had undertaken the marriage bond in the chapel of Ard late last evening. And now, finding no comfort in her mother's mild words, her father's boozy cajolery, her husband's bland imperturbability, or in the chatter of her female in-laws friendly and sly, she went down into the kitchen to the group of her old neighbours who had come from Ard with the wedding party.

The dancing-barn outside had been for some time deserted and the kitchen was now thronged with people who fell silent when she appeared. Wheezing beerladen breaths, trails of tobacco smoke, specks of sand from the concrete floor floating in a frostfog — all this made the silence a palpable thing confronting her, a phantom, to try and drag from her the words that would express the anguish of her being. It was that time of a wedding morning when a man might go about starting a row and find none to hinder him. The fire had gone out of the drunken voices, the laughter was lifeless. The young folk, it seemed to her, got up without much heart to dance the jig, afraid that the married couples and oldtimers might take advantage of the quiet that was beginning to close in about the house and say it was time to go. Even the young folk from Ard, hardened to revelling and constant labour, every one of them by now was bleary of voice, weary of foot. The only one in the house left with some flinty fire in his footwork and the flush of life in his cheek was Beairtlin, her father's servant-boy.

Nora dropped her head and let that flintspark penetrate her mind, that flush invade her being, till the silence and the unhomely thing receded. She remembered the many spells of innocent courting with him, snatching dulse from him in summer, or in the autumn the two of them on the flags of the dooryard cracking the nuts he had brought her from the hazelgrove of Liss, and nights of fireside chat together when the old couple were gone to bed and she was waiting up for Padraig her brother to come home from a visit. The girls of Ard, who were at the wedding tonight, had often given her a sly dig suggesting Beairtlin for her. Tonight was the one night none of them would think of him for her, but it was the one night she wouldn't have minded. Beairtlin's witty remarks, that's what used take the bitter edge off her laughter whenever her father and mother were settling a match for her. A pain of regret, dulled not healed. That she had been so slow to speak her mind to him that day, so unwilling to find fault with Providence, when Beairtlin told her that 'the old fellow was making a match for her again, and no one would be given a wisp of consideration except a shopkeeper or a boss-man of the Plain'.

It wasn't because she had been vexed with Beairtlin for

what he said that she passed remarks that day about his hare-lip. Instead, she had intended to say that she'd go off warm and willing with him there and then. For when all is said and done, it wasn't his slim and shapely person, his skygrey eye, his cheek red as foxglove, no, it was the hare-lip, that disfigurement he was marked with from the womb — he didn't even try to hide it with a moustache — that attracted her eyes and her passionate lips. It attracted and repelled her, often her disgust got the upper hand, too often, that's what left the web of her young life a heap of grey dust today. Even now it was the hare-lip she saw coming at her like a bloodsucking lamprey through a grey sea-lough. Beairtlin grumbed that 'the Plainers had taken over the house all night with their reel sets', but she couldn't attend to him till the pair of them were out on the middle of the floor dancing the plain set of home.

—So you're spancelled at last? he said humorously, appearing to hide his vexation.

—God willing, she answered. She realised fully for the first time what neither match, marriage nor the wedding itself had given her clearly to understand.

—Have no regrets. You've made a good swap, lashings and leavings and being your own mistress here on the level Plain, in place of the rocks and the slave-labour — and not to mention the vigilant eye of your old fellow — out at Ardbeg. We'll send you an odd cargo of dulse, an odd bottle of poteen, and a bundle of nuts in the autumn.

Nora's heart missed a beat. She had forgotten until now that there was no dulse, no nuts, no poteen here.

—I spent last night looking for you, Beairtlin, to sing *The Deer's Wood by Casla* for me, but there wasn't a sight of you in the crowd. You'll sing it after this dance. Do. I'm longing to hear it again . . .

But Beairtlin had hardly cleared his throat for the song when her mother and her husband's sister came and carried her off again to the parlour.

—Time for us to be home, said the mother. Look, it's broad daylight, and your husband Martin here without sleep since the night before last. You two are at home,

God bless you, but look at the journey we have before us.

—Eleven miles to Gaalwaay, said Martin Ryan, the new husband. He had a slow congealed kind of a voice and the unhomely accent of the Plain. —And fifteen miles farther west again, isn't that it? That's what he used to tell me, a labouring man I had here one year from Ard.

Despite their talk of the long miles and the scurry there was for coats and shawls, Nora wouldn't admit that her family and friends were leaving her. She was made realise it when the Ardbeg girls came kissing her and saying 'not to be homesick, they'd slip over an odd time on a visit'. She recognised every individual shout of the Ardbeg boys going wildly on their bikes back down the Galway road, and that left the Plainsfolk more alien than ever as they took leave of her in the misty morning light. And all with their 'Missus Ryan' so pat on the tongue causing her cold shivers of fear. The cars that had brought the Ardbeg people were humming out on the road, the drivers hooting the horns. As she had done so many times before at the end of a wedding Nora put on her overcoat and walked out to the road. Beairtlin was the last one to crush into the car that held her family.

—It's God's will, Beairtlin, she said. Keep me a handful of dulse.

Beairtlin had fixed the cape-ends of his raincoat across his mouth. Though her senses swam she caught the meaning in his words which came squeezed out through the hare-lip opening. —Don't worry. And I'll bring you a bag of nuts too. In the autumn.

—There's plenty of noots in the cregs hereabouts, said her husband standing alongside her.

She stood unmoving at the gate looking after the car until it had passed Crossroads rise, pretending not to have heard her mother's parting words, 'not to be homesick, she'd see them soon again.'

Homesick? That anchor, keeping the spirit though in exile fixed in its native harbour? No, she wasn't homesick. Tossed on a wave's crest at the caprice of God, having cut her life's cable, not a single link left with her natural element since Beairtlin went, she drove on straight ahead like a boat that has lost its bearings to the Crossways rise. She had never been nearer than Galway to this district and it had been dark during the wedding-drive last night, still it wasn't to view the country that she walked to the crest of this hill. Her only idea was to climb the first rise that came her way and get out of this smothering trough between the two waves of past and present. At that moment she couldn't tell whether Martin Ryan was to the left or right of her, she took no interest in the stem of his pipe circling the prominent points while he himsèlf stabbed the queer uncouth names in the face of her illwill and detestation. She didn't notice Ryan leaving her and going back to the house.

The fog was being rolled and thinned out and dragged by a freshening wind in grey diminishing strips to the edge of the Plain. As far as her eye could see, nothing but immense flat fields, no stones, no rock-heaps, and every foot of fencing as straight as a fishing-line except where they were submerged in winter flooding. Here and there a stand of trees, a thicket, down below her a few outcrops of bedrock like knots in a deal table that had been bleached and scoured. The spot where she stood was the most airy hill of all the dull rich expanse. The houses were not strung together here, the nearest wavering thread of smoke seemed to her a mile away. All the houses alike. And the same set of trees sheltering the walls of the haggards. It appeared to her fancy that one immense house had split in the night and all its parts had separated as far as they might out of sheer unneighbourliness. She looked back at her husband's house. Not too unlike her father's house in make and appearance, two-storey, slated. But her father's house had looked newer, with a view of the sea, bare hills at the back of it, the house itself seeming a section of granite sliced out of the rock country to be set up as some tall symbolic stone in the middle of the group of thatched houses called Ardbeg. But there was a greater difference still. The two houses were as different as chalk from cheese. Like all the surrounding countryside her new house had a certain stupid arrogance, it reminded her of the smug smile of a shop-keeper examining his bankbook. Boasting to her face that it was no mushroom growth but a part of the everlasting. She knew it was a 'warm' house. She knew her father wouldn't have set her there if it wasn't, in view of her dowry and all the well-heeled upstarts he had refused on her behalf. She shivered to think that from now on she would be simply one of the conveniences among the conveniences of this house.

Here there was no barrier of mountain and sea to restrain a rambling foot or limit a wandering imagination. Nothing but the smooth monotonous Plain to absorb one's yearnings and privacies and weave them into the one drab undifferentiated fabric, as each individual drop, whatever its shade, whatever its nature before being engulfed in the womb of it, the ocean transmutes into its own grey phantom face. From now on whatever contact she'd have with home would be only a thin thread in this closeknit stuff.

There was a chilliness in the morning, not a genuine cold — rather like the friendliness of her sisters-in-law. She went in. She noticed there was nothing out of place within. After all the merrymaking the kitchen wasn't disordered enough to be called homely, not to say Irish. Their own kitchen at home had often been more of a shambles after a couple of hours dancing during a neighbourly visit. Apart from the two tables set end to end in the parlour, the attendants had set everything to rights before they went, and there wasn't the slightest thing crooked to mark that an event had taken place, that two lives had been spiritually and bodily woven together in the tie of intercourse under the one roof to ensure the spring of life in that house. The prime events of a man's destiny skimmed across the wide placid surface of this countryside as lightly as a finger-stone is flicked across water.

Sitting she looked about the kitchen, it was the first chance she had got of examining it since she came to the house. There were signs of careful housekeeping, nursing things to last long, on every single item from the saucepans cleaned and scoured to the two tall presses blond and mellow. A burial chamber, the image might have occurred, vessels and furniture set in it never to be moved until time should undo them; but, ignorant of the antiquities, what she did ask herself was how Ryan all on his own had kept the place so spick and span. This house needed no woman's hand. Strangest of all, neither hearth nor fire to be seen. Instead there was a metal range, dull and unwelcoming, the last spark had died somewhere within its womb.

—I wonder where's the turf? she said to herself getting up. In order to change this alien cold into a warm intimacy she must heap up a fire that would make the iron range red hot and prove to herself that a warm fire was more than a match for the rigid iron.

—I use nothing but coal, he said. Wouldn't it be better not bother with a fire and take a lie-down on the bed?

She took fright. Till now she hadn't thought of the bed. That drowsy voice, assured, self-assertive, set up waves of repulsion in her, yet she recognised it as the voice of authority, not to be denied if he felt like bringing the thing to a head.

—I'm not sleepy, she said at last. But her husband had gone out for the coal. He soon returned and shot a shovelful of it into the maw of the range. His jabs with the poker at the embers got on Nora's nerves. Like a soul gripped by the demon on the edge of desire, the embers were quickly breaking apart and trying to flame. She'd give anything if her husband's father, mother, any of his prating sisters or even a silent one, were here at the hearth.

The smoke of Ryan's pipe was rising up to the loft in measured puffs, unruffled, unconcerned. The smoke of her father's pipe, or Beairtlin's, always made twists and angles as if they were wrestling with something in the air. There were none of the unfenced regions of her homeland in her husband's conversation, none of the wild oats of speech. Prosy and precise, he could hardly be otherwise, for his mind was a smooth plain without the slightest up or down from end to end . . . With his rare attempts at a joke, a smile crinkling the stiff crease of his nose, he reminded her of the god of wisdom trying to be merry a minute. The more she grew accustomed to the local accent the more alien she felt it. She longed for a new twist in the tune — a change of person, change of day, change of time, that it might be night again, or that his voice might be angry, anything but that gentle deadly drone that did nothing now but linger in her ears.

She got up and stood in the doorway in the fresh air. Plump hens just let out were already scrabbling in the flowerbeds on each side of the concrete path that led from the steps at the front gate. What scant flowers had already poked up through the earth had been trampled last night. There was Beairtlín's footprint — how could she mistake it, the many times it had caught her eye, on the bog, in the earth, on the seasand. She was examining the shape of the boot when a heavyfoot man with the soft hat of the region and a cord breeches passed on the road. Nora remembered he was some neighbour of her husband's, he had been given special treatment in the parlour last night. Without slowing his step and with only the slightest turn of his head her way he greeted her briefly. Sparing his words as if every syllable was worth another penny towards the rent. The fog had come down again in a drab shawl over the Plain with only odd slits of visibility. Still she wouldn't have gone back in so quickly if a filthy hen hadn't angered her by scratching away the footprint with a mindless claw from the soft impressionable earth . . .

She sat again in the same chair by the range. With the heat of the fire and the weariness her husband was asleep and snoring — a dull measured snore peaceful and passionless. The gentle ripple of a languid sea on the shingle in a summer calm. She studied him for the first time as she might some insignificant item of her new life. Long limbs, angular shoulders. Centuries of sun and shower, soil and drudgery, had shaped and marked that robust body, the sinewy neck, the sallow features. A black head of hair edged with grey, sign of strength. Lids shut on those slow dull eyes in which she could imagine neither smile of pleasure nor flash of anger nor the soft haze of desire. Flaring nostrils that wouldn't be too squeamish of smells.

A sootblack moustache — she had caught it out of the corner of her eye a few times previously and felt it needed badly to be cut. And now particularly, realising that those thick seal's bristles weren't hiding a hare-lip.

Floodtide

Mairead shook herself, made a fork of her first and ring-finger to rub the sleepclots from her eyes, felt the early-morning chill on her forearms. Her body took pleasure in her failure to rise. She curled herself back again on the warm side of the bed which Padraig had left a short while ago.

The month since she had come home, together with the three weeks since she had married, had left her out of practice. She thought of those ten years in America when she used to be out on the floor every single morning at the first clockwarning before daybreak for the sake of . . . for the sake of this day — a day when she could either rise or lie abed as she liked.

—Did ye get up yet? The quavering voice of her mother-in-law, it reached her from the far-room through the door which Padraig had left open behind him.

—We did, said Mairead, and rubbed some more sleep out of her eyes.

They said, she told herself, that Padraig wouldn't have the tenacity to wait for me until I'd be able to pay their passages over for my three sisters. It was said that since he was 'the only eye in the spud' he would give in to his mother and marry some other woman long ago . . . It was said that considering how young I was when I went over I'd forget him, marry beyond, and likely . . .

—Get up, Mairead. Lydon will be fit to be tied. The ebb

won't wait for anybody . . .

She was jerked out of her daydream by the sharpness which she sensed for the first time in the old woman's voice. It proclaimed that the immemorial duel between a man's mother and his wife was about to begin. Having fastened on the bits of clothes that were nearest to her hand in the halfdark she remembered the rumour that was going the rounds, that the old woman was irked by the scant dowry which she had brought into the house. To wait ten years . . . Put up with a member of the American upper-class and the crumbs that fell from the table . . . Her shoe-lace broke in half in the second eyelet from the bottom . . . She felt the first tinge of bitterness.

—It's a long time since anyone got up so early in this house! Spring is at hand, at long last. Now Mairead, a splash of tea would make a gay young man of me.

Padraig had a fire down, the kettle hissing on the boil, while he brought a handful of oats out to the horse that stood already straddled at the door. With the gaiety in his voice, the love and affection that showed in his face as he named her, Mairead's irritation melted away. For the sake of all this she'd be well able to bear with the old woman's nagging. There'd never be an angry word between herself and Padraig, or if there was she herself would surely be to blame . . .

It wasn't quite bright as they left home. Down at the Beach Boreen Lydon's two daughters were seated on a pair of upturned basket-creels, while Lydon himself strode up and down at the edge of the shingle gnawing on his pipe.

—Upon my oath, he said, damn the wisp of seaweed I thought'd be cut on the Ridge today! I never yet saw a new-married couple destroyed by a desire to get up.

The pair of daughters smiled, and Mairead laughed aloud.

—It has ebbed a bit, said Padraig sheepishly.

—Ebbed a bit! And it almost at low-water! The spring-tide is at the second day of its strength, and unless we seize our chance, today and tomorrow, there'll be no such

low-water again this year when it'll be possible to reap the
deep seaweed beds of the Ridge.

—It's a spring-tide, said Mairead innocently. Having gone
to America so early in life she had only a hazy knowledge
of some of the home realities whose names were knit into
the network of her memory.

—Spring-tide, said Lydon with the look of a bishop in
whose presence an impudent blasphemy has been uttered.
—The Spring-tide of the Feast of St Brigit! You're not
acclimatised to the spring-tides yet, girl dear, and they're
not exactly what's itching you.

He winked an eye at her and with a beck of his head
drew her attention to Padraig who was on ahead, going
down the shingle slope with Mairead's creel fixed into his
own slung from his back.

At this point she didn't feel much like talk, it was
enough to have to envisage her share of today's work which
lay before her. For a week past the old couple had but the
one tune, the Spring-tide. But she hadn't been a bit worried
about going to the beach until she found herself now at
the edge of the shingle.

She was born and grew up on 'Great Harbour's edge'.
She had gathered periwinkles and sandeels, sloke, dulse,
carrageen. The spring before she crossed over she had
helped her father cut beach-crop. But she had gone before
she was fully inured to the hardship of the shore. Soon her
hands were wrinkled with washing, scouring, cooking,
instead of acquiring the leathery skin of the sea-forager.
Those ten years — years in which the sea would have
injected its own bitterness into her blood and tempered
her bones to its own mettle — she had spent them without
setting eyes above ten times on saltwater.

But as they came then to the exposed margin of the
ocean the salt wind in from the great waste sharpened her
spirit.

—Aren't there many in the neighbourhood, she said to
herself, many who spent even twenty years in America and
are as used to this hardship today as if they had never left
home? What's the hardship of the sea but part of the

hardship I'll have to school myself again to? How is it worse than bog-hardship, field-hardship, the hardship of cattle and pigs, the hardship of bearing and rearing if God grants me family . . .

At the same time she would have preferred if that section of seaweed on the Ridge wasn't to be gathered in partnership with the Lydons. Would Nora and Caitin Lydon be mocking the ignoramus? Would the tale of her clumsiness come home to her mother-in-law? —How well it happened on my first day out that the Ridge had to be harvested in partnership! Pity it's not myself alone and Padraig.

She was determined to do her best for Padraig's sake, but she knew the best he'd allow her would be little enough for fear she'd overstrain herself from lack of practice in the job. If there were only two potatoes in the cow's tub it was —For God's sake, your back! from Padraig. Just now Mairead would rather he threw his shyness to the wind and wait to give her a helping hand. She was having great difficulty with the smooth and shifting stones of the shingle which were sliding under her feet and twice as quick to slip the more she tried to tread lightly over them.

—There's a vast difference between this and the streets of New York, said Lydon as they clattered down to the end of the shingle. —You should have put on hobnailed boots. You'd do better on the beach barefoot than in those light little toytoys.

—First thing to my hand this morning, said Mairead laughing, this time with an effort.

The sand, crisp and firm, on the ebb-strand was such a relief that she made a short dash towards a cluster of whelks and periwinkles which the tide had left stranded overnight. She inserted the toe of her shoe under them and struck Padraig with them on the calf of the leg. But he still didn't wait back for her.

She found it hard going at the place they called 'the footway' between high-water mark and the farthest line of the ebb. Every year, every generation, Lydons and Cades had planned to make a horse-track of this, but it remained

'intention good, performance poor'. She made a good deal
of this uncouth passage by taking little leaps clean across
the pools. Whenever she was faced with rugged outcrops of
rock she slid sideways along them embracing a boulder.
Her paps and the rockgrowths both suffered. Once a tentacle
of sea-anemone kept her from falling. Once a little kingdom
of periwinkles on a rockface went splashing down into the
pool. The laughter of the work-party echoed in the clefts
and fissures of the shore.

The Ridge was the farthest point out from land: a reef
of rock, gapped, polished and bitten into by the ceaseless
gnawing of the ocean. The Ridge was never entirely exposed;
yet it could be harvested at the ebb of a spring-tide if one
took the chance of a wetting. Padraig tucked the ends of
his jacket of white homespun into his trouser-band and
went to his hips in the narrow channel, but drew back
again when he felt himself taken.

—We had better start on this black-weed here, Lydon
said as if venting his ill-humour with the Cades in redirect-
ing it against the slowness of the ebb. —Isn't that a nuisance
now?

—Not worth our while killing ourselves with a year's
growth, said Padraig, but since everyone else had begun
he started himself. It pained Mairead to see the saltwater
dripping from his clothes. She glanced towards him again
and again so that the look in her eye might let him know
how sorry she felt for him, but Padraig never once raised
his head. She understood that since the spoils were to be
divided equally between the two households, and seeing
that there were three Lydons, Padraig was attempting to
do two men's work. It didn't take her long to realise he
was actually standing in for three: she herself was useless,
might as well not be there at all. She was slipping on the
slimy rockslabs, while the scabby one-year's growth was so
tough that she skinned her knuckles trying to strip it from
the rough coating of the stones. No matter how often she
sharpened her hack-knife the result was the same. A stalk
of seaweed sliced her finger. She stared at the blood dripping
on the rock, loth to complain. Until Caitin Lydon noticed

it and bound it with a strip of her calico bodice which the saltwater took neatly off again in no time. She felt her fingers numb, dark blue blotches appeared about the joints on the back of her hands. She had to begin rubbing the back of one hand in the crotch of the other. But she wasn't really shamed until she had to go wading.

Padraig glanced at her now and then out of the corner of his eye, vexation in his look, she thought — vexed that on account of the partnership she was obliged to do work which for his part he'd never ask her to do.

—The February bite is in the morning yet, said Caitin Lydon. I suppose you find the beach strange?

—Ah, not very, said Mairead. One has to get used to it I suppose.

—It's a sloppy sort of earning, said Nora Lydon. If I was in America, Lord, it's long 'ere I'd leave it. My passage is coming this summer.

—You're never without the hard and belittling word for the life at home, said Caitin to her young sister. But perhaps you may sigh for it some day.

Caitin spoke in the adult tone of a housewife, heir to the Lydon house, land and strand. But it seemed to Mairead that somewhat more than the mere defence of the homelife caused the sting in her voice. It was on the tip of Mairead's tongue to tell her about the shopkeeper in Brooklyn who had been pressing her to marry him until the day she left America; however, she refrained. It would be a matter for mockery in all the visiting-houses of the village that night. Did ever a slut or a slattern come back from America who hadn't some millionaire or other asking to marry her beyond?

By now the men had succeeded in getting out on the Ridge by going waist-deep in the water but the women stayed where they were until it had ebbed more in the channel.

Lydon, out on the Ridge, kept up a constant stream of orders back to his own daughers — strip the stones down to the skin — they wouldn't be reaped again for a couple of years. But Mairead was well aware he was aiming at her, though his eye never once lit on her. Soon the women moved out across the channel towards a red sand newly exposed near the last of the ebb. Mairead stood watching a crab that flopped about in a pool till he went in under a slanting stone. It gave her her best to dislodge the stone, but what came out of it but a tiny speckled fish that escaped her grasp and went into a cleft between two thighs of rock. Her heart jerked. She thought of the lusty appetite for crabs and rockfish she had when a girl. Her father had never come home from a seaweed-strand without bringing back some beach-gatherings. If Padraig wasn't so busy she'd ask him to collect her a hank of crabs and rockfish. The slab beside her was architected all over with limpets. She had a keen thought of the rare occasions she had served limpets and cockles as a tasty titbit in America, but she wouldn't give tuppence for that manner of serving compared with a batch of shellfish roasted on the embers. She began to long for the limpets. Maybe, too, they might sweeten the humour of the old woman at home. She thrust her blade in under the edge of a limpet that was slightly detached from the stone. She was reluctant at first to interfere between it and the rock. In spite of herself she was thinking of her mother-in-law going between herself and Padraig. But the limpet came away so readily with her that she had no further scruple. Pity I haven't a little can or a bucket, she thought. Then she remembered the apron she had on over her American dress, if she gathered it up and tied it behind it would hold a fine lot. She could put them in the creel when work on the beach was over. Bit by bit, she told herself, I am getting the knack of the shore.

—It's not worth bothering yourself with those limpets, Mairead, said Lydon. —There's twice the sustenance in the top-shore limpet than in the low-water one, and anyhow the limpet is never at his prime till he has taken three drinks of April water.

Though what he said was true, she took the hint that it wasn't to pick limpets she came but to cut seaweed.

She made her way out farther along with the two women.

She was attracted by the little sand-pools left by the last of the ebb. Her thoughts were seduced by the faint thrum of the wave in the channel-mouth and the ripples of brine breaking in white flakes on the miniature strand made her happy in herself so that she lay into the work. Nor did she find it so piercingly difficult. Though the commonest weed here was the sawtooth wrack there was a lush growth of black-weed here and there on the backs of the jagged scarps, with patches of top-shore seaweed in among it and luxurious bunches of yellow-weed that were like golden tresses of hair in the rays of the morning sun. She was keener to go at them than she had been with the limpets a short while ago.

Now Lydon's tone began to grow sharp:

—Of course, ladies, ye don't imagine that old coarse-crop field of mine back up there is able to digest sawtooth wrack! Every single stalk of it will be still in the earth in its own shape next autumn. It isn't as if I'd ask you your business if it was sowing the loam at the bottom of the village I was. The tidewater is shallow enough now for you to come out here.

Caitin Lydon went out barefoot as far as a boulder under the Ridge. Nora took her boots off and got out on to another a slab. Mairead did likewise with her own boots. About to hoist up her skirt she hesitated once or twice and glanced shamefaced towards Lydon and Padraig. All she had under it was a transparent American petticoat. It surprised her at first how unconcerned the other pair were about hoisting a skirt, until she remembered they had never left home. Her feet shrank from the cold water, she went as gingerly as a cat crossing a patch of wet.

Suddenly she was afraid, the turbulent sea breaking in white spume over the lip of rock in the channel might sweep her legs from under her. The soles of her feet tingled on the gravelly bottom. She tensed her lips, it seemed to her the Lydons were grinning. She looked longingly out towards Padraig, he had his back to her, shearing as furiously as chance offered in the maw of the wave. He never as much as lifted his head . . .

She was out now on the exposed Ridge in face of the beds of strapwrack. The rank fronds of it excited her greed. She felt a lust to plunder. A desire to strip the rockfaces clean as a plate. She took pleasure in the squeak of the long ribbons of it letting go their hold and the hiss of the sheaves falling in the rock hollows. In spite of the chill and drench of the saltwater she felt a prick in her pulse, a prick ten years absent . . . She came to a gentle nook sheltered in under the backbone of the Ridge, where there was a feathery growth of carrageen on the cheek of the stone. How often that tuft of carrageen which Nora Sheain Liam brought to America had sent her thoughts bounding to 'Great Habour's edge', to the dear beach where lay her heart's desire . . . Again remembering her mother-in-law, she turned aside to pick the carrageen.

—Ladies, said Lydon, and now the ocean's urgency was in his voice, you are proving yourselves none too good. This reef isn't half-reaped yet. How shy you are of wetting yourselves! Saltwater never did harm to anybody.

Mairead gave up the carrageen, though the voice of Lydon caused her no irritation now. Now she felt sure she was fit to do her share, sure that the ocean's temper was getting under her own skin and through her veins the harsh reality was pulsing.

Again came the warning voice of Lydon:

—It's on the turn! Look, Carrigavackin almost submerged. Hadn't the ladies better begin drawing? They're more suited to that just now.

For the first time today Padraig raised his head and looked Mairead in the eye. He was on the verge of saying something, but shut his lips up tight again without speaking. Mairead understood, clearly he would forbid her that labour if he could. The strong bond of the partnership had inhibited the affection showing in his eye that moment. He needn't worry. She intended to show that though she might appear to be soft-spun there was a tough weft in her too. Since he was so good to her she was going to put herself to the limit for his sake.

They began filling from the part farthest out. They'd

still be able to collect the nearer part until the tide had come well in.

For hands that had been ten years in the sweltering heat of a narrow kitchen it was pure refreshment to feel the stiff slime of the seaweed sticking to them as she stuffed the creel full to the brim. She had no great difficulty with the first creel in spite of the ruggedness of the passage while the brine streamed from the seaweed down along her back.

She put as much top-load on the second creel as did either of the Lydons. Very likely she wouldn't have slipped only that a sheaf of the top-load which overhung the edge of the creel slid off as she cleared the end of the Ridge. But though she slipped she wasn't injured. She grasped a rock which was right at her back and kept such a grip on the creel that only a few sheaves fell off the top. She would have preferred if the two Lydons had gone on instead of leaving their creels on the stones and coming back to help her gather the fallen sheaves. After the third creel it seemed to her that the Lydons were dawdling to allow her to keep up. The spreading-bank was nine or ten yards above highwater mark; the plod up there from the low-water edge seemed to grow longer with every creel. Like trying to teem out a fulltide, she thought.

She was sweating all over, felt the warm trickles of sweat tempering the chill of the saltwater. The strap began to raise blisters on her palms, the brine was biting into the crease of her fingers. Her back was bent stiff, and as for her legs, well, better forget them. They seemed to belong to someone else, not the legs of the one who had come down the boreen so quick and lithe that morning. Afraid every minute she'd turn an ankle. The soles had lifted clean from her light shoes. Every time she trod on a sharp pebble she clenched her foot, arching the instep against the shoe-laces. She was like a horse with a nail in the quick lifting her foot from a pointed periwinkle or a limpet shell. She was also ravenously hungry. She hadn't eaten much that morning. For ten years she had been in the habit of a cup of tea in the hand at eleven o'clock every day. But fasting was child's play in comparison with this excruciating work.

In America there was a break or a change of occupation after every stint. But the selfsame journey, from low-water to the top of the beach, again and again . . .

Lydon's temper was shortening step by step with the rising tide.

—You are slow, ladies! It seems we'll have to leave this reef uncut and go drawing ourselves. If we're depending on you the floodtide will take a share of what we've already cut.

Once the men began drawing the pace grew fiercer. The rugged beach didn't cost them a thought, no more than it did Caitin Lydon who was able to keep up with them barefoot step for step. More often than not Padraig was emptying his creel on the spread-bank by the time the others had reached the tidemark, with Mairead still not beyond the edge of the sand.

There was no feeling left in her feet. Sometimes when she came to the upper edge of the sand she shut her eyes awhile so as not to be pierced by the prospect of the final stretch. She was dead to all sense of pain by now. She plodded along as if there was someone inside her goading her on. If her body was numb her mind was more so. Nothing occurred to her except disconnected scraps of thought . . . the partnership . . . if the seaweed was left to Padraig and myself . . . a body must become inured to the hardship . . . the floodtide . . .

She slackened now on the slope of the shingle without strength or will to open her eyes properly. First thing she knew she was into the tidemark, the heap of shells and periwinkles, oozy tangles of oarweed root, bits of board encrusted with barnacles, ringlets of wrack and trash-heaps of red seaweed which had come up with the full of the spring-tide from where it had been rotting during the neap. It was on a slimy strand of redweed she slipped. Quite aware of the feet sliding from under her, she let them go. A relief to let the strap of the creel slip from her grasp . . . Padraig refilled the creel, took it to the finish.

The eyes of the Lydon girls seemed to her to smile, in

spite of what they had to say of . . . treacherous stones . . . too long a distance . . .

To think she had left the comfort of America for the sake of this. Yet Padraig wasn't to blame for it.

—No need for you to go down any more, Mairead, said Lydon. The three of us will gather what's left out there at a single go, and it'll be no trouble to your boss-man to gather a little creel of the floating weed down at the channel. Padraig lad, hurry, the flood won't have a clump left.

But now Mairead was determined to go back down. How well they wouldn't ask Nora or Caitin Lydon to stay up here? She'd go down if only to spite them. If that floating weed contained only a single clump she'd make two halves of that clump! She had made her bed and she'd lie on it . . .

In spite of his striding haste she kept up with Padraig on the way down and when they reached low-tide mark she was no more out of breath than he was. It was some satisfaction that she had Padraig to herself for the first time since they had come to the beach. She gave up the idea of gathering her share of the floating weed into her own creel: there wasn't the full of a creel in it all told.

Floodtide was now so fiercely breaking in that it seemed to regret having been caught out that morning and intended to take full revenge for having bared at all. It pushed into the channel nuzzling the little piles of stones with its cold snout, sniffing into fissures with its nostrils hissing, feeling its way far up along the ebbway of red sand with its long greedy tentacles, making ravenous attacks on the cut swathes of weed not yet collected. It had already taken a few substantial heaps and Padraig was put to his knees trying to save a clump of strapweed from its gullet.

The rage and rapacity of the sea was in tune with Mairead's turbulent mood. The rush of the surf was an ease to her agonised spirit as it tousled the sawtooth wrack on the stones and broke them despondently, not having yet displaced the little pad of sand the ebb had left. But hardly had the little scattered rills of the first wave been absorbed by the sand when the thrust of the next wave was come to dislodge the wee strip once and for all. Mairead stood in a cold pool on bare-strand edge till the reflux of the wave which had taken the sand-pad drenched her up to the knees. A swimming-crab came out of a crevice and went foraging down the sloping shoulders of the wave. A periwinkle went from the rock as if in a game of tip-and-come with the upsurge of seawater which made a rush for the last gatherings of weed. Out went Mairead into the mouth of the surf to retrieve a clump — a glistening clump of yellow-weed.

—Out of my way! said Padraig and went to his thighs to snatch the last of the plunder from the devouring tide. Mairead straightened, her mind flared up at that voice. A harsh alien voice. A voice from a law of life other than the life of his complaining letters, other than the life of beguiling and sweethearting, alien to the life of the pillow. With the stab she got the little bladder of seaweed burst between her fingers and squirted a dull slime up in her cheek.

The dark shade she saw on Padraig's features at that moment was as strange and forbidding as the black streaks which the freshening wind was making in the bristling mane of the floodtide . . .

Going On

Only her selfdenial overcoming her hunger kept her from biting a mouthful of the tough burnt crust for herself. And it wasn't the eyes of the six-year-old, fixed and frightened, that caused her to abstain, but the wasted hand which the youngster extended between crust and mouth to take hold of a life that was slipping from him before he had a chance to get a grip on it. She set the halfmug of milk, the whole of the morning's milking, on the table-edge beside her husband. He merely glanced sideways out of inflamed eyes at the mug-handle, spat a tough phlegm into the fire, opened the door and went out in the yard. She let the youngster snatch at the milk, being troubled by the look in the man's eye as he drew the door to behind him. She listened a moment to the gulped milk gurgling in the avid young gullet. She was about to tell him the crust would be tastier if he dipped it in the milk, but found it not worth the trouble, there was so little milk left, so little crust. She hadn't made the effort to tell him at the start, it would have been less difficult to tell him then than tell him now. Her tongue was as dry as the skin of a bellows.

She took a fistful of oats from the bottom of the bin, shook it on the floor, opened the wicker coop in the corner, forgetting till she had called 'chuck, chuck' and there was no answering cackle that they had gnawed the bones of the last hen the day before. Going out for a can of water her mind stayed as if it were fixated in yesterday in a way quite beyond her control. By the doorstep on the way back she left the can on the goose-pen opposite the wall of the Well Garth as she used always do coming with a can in each hand. She was unable to keep her mind from thinking was it yesterday or a week earlier or a month ago that the last geese were in that pen. With the way things were for three months now weeks and days intermingled blanking each other out in the confusion of her mind, she was on her hunkers and had opened the little slot of the pen before recollecting that there couldn't be any geese in there. Her man was sloping off from the manureheap to the byre door, a torn strip hung from the tail of his white homespun jacket, dungstained, as if some wandering evil thing had clung to it. Unpinning the doorlatch he glanced briefly at the yard and for a second his tormented eyes met those of his wife. But the agony in his eyes left her untouched. For a moment she lost thought of who he was, forgot they were married, lived together. At the same time she knew he was going in for the donkey, to harness it, bring a load of manure to the potato-field at the top of the village as he did every morning. She was on the point of telling him there was no need to put that labour on himself since they had no seed potatoes left, but why should she bother, he knew it well.

She poured the water into the small pot and hung it over the fire for no reason except that she had been in the habit of boiling a mess of cabbagestalks for the hens at that time every morning. No sooner had she the pot on than she remembered she had neither a hen nor a pullet left. She went out to drive the cow down to the Shore Garth as she always did after getting the youngster ready for school. She found the man in the byre, he had let the donkey loose in the yard. He came from the donkey's corner to loose the cow also. Unusual for him, it was he who had tied the cow the night before, making a tight knot instead of her own running loop. The knot was too tight, instead of loosening it he slipped the halter off the tie-stick altogether and threw it up over a crossbeam along with the donkey's halter until it would be wanted again in the evening. Neither paid the least regard to the other. She had a distinct idea that the man used to be gone from the yard by that time each morning. But before another glimmer of understanding came — no need to sow — the whole situation had ebbed from her mind.

As always she kept pace with the cow who knew her own way down to the Shore Garth. Approaching the highway she remembered she had put the pot on and never replenished the fire under it. And she hadn't got the youngster ready for school. She tried to hurry and at once her mind became a cauldron of water over a blazing fire boiling with stinging bubbles of ideas, school, youngster, the little pot, the cow, rising up one after another here and there. These pricked other upstarts of memory. The fair. Her credit run out. All the time hiding her distress from the neighbours. The seed gone. The Flour Committee that was promised. Never came. And the Poorhouse. Then the blobs of memory became so confused that she failed to distinguish one from the other and she pushed on.

The cow's pace was more lackadaisical than ever this morning but she made no attempt to urge her on. Even coming out on to the highway when the horn of a car blew a long warning blast both cow and herself remained unhurried crossing to reach the track to the shore before the car might come on top of them. Surrounded by the wind of the car, brakes whining by the cow's chest, she was jerked into an unwanted awareness. If the car killed the cow with the fair only two days off? For the first time it occurred to her, suppose they killed the cow themselves and ate her? They'd be dead before fair-day after a whole six months of distress and misery. She tried to consider this idea, but it was like trying to thread a tiny needle-eye with strands too thick and too many at once, so many thoughts were getting in each other's way no single one would penetrate. Her understanding was limp, crippled not so much by the morning fast itself as by the everpresent thought of it, and the thought of her credit, the Committee, the fair, cow, supper, breakfast. And since she had failed altogether to provide for this morning her mind could

now be let disintegrate. An old boat on the harbour bottom
having put its last load ashore.

A great ease now, all emotion cut out of her, her feelings
dulled. Whenever she tried to think that fit of freedom
invaded her body. Began as a flame in her womb. Incited
her palate and tongue with prickles of thirst. Broke in a
soft blob from her forehead sending ideas floating like a
shower of bubbles before her eyes. Her bodily senses were
in sharp conflict as if only the most tenacious one among
them was due to survive. At times she thought all the
sounds of the world were in her ears so that she failed to
distinguish a familiar sound amongst them. Other times her
hearing went altogether dead, replaced by a vision, bound-
less, impersonal, with nothing precisely to see, no item of
interest. Then it was taste came spurting up till the salt
tang of every sea was on the tip of her tongue and all
hives' honeycombs . . .

It was a pleasant morning in late February. The earth
smelled good. Big buds breaking on the tree. Juicy green
leaves on shrubs and thornbrakes leaning across the walls.
The mating call of a blackbird, a lone lamb bleating, floodtide at the full thudding on the shingle: some kindly creative
force giving bodily shape to its word in the incarnation of
virgin Nature. But for the woman it was a world remote
from human senses. A world without beauty, sweet smell,
sound or taste. A world without length or breadth or
thickness, insubstantial, insensitive. A world with no
mystique and no evangel, with neither birth-certificate nor
final fields. It seemed a world that was casting off its old
familiar traits while powerless to put on new appearances.

She didn't chew a grassblade, a juicy leaf or hawthorn
bud, as she used to do with relish every morning up to
this. She used linger too at the gap into the Shore Garth.
Every morning driving the cow in at the gap she'd go
plucking cress in the waterdykes by the boundary walls.
Here too she used to take a shortcut by night to dig up
some of the early seed-potatoes they had in Little Plot
and boil them unknown to her man. There was still cress in
the dykes, there were drills still untouched in Little Plot,

but she had neither enough relish of life nor enough energy to gather them. After a time she gave the cow a light slap of her palm and pushed on.

On to the Shore Garth with the cow, as she did yesterday, the day before that, a week ago. Shore Garth, it was fixed in her mind and being, along with the fair, the mealtimes she could remember, the times she had to go without eating. The cow ambled, tearing tufts from the wayside grass, munching one half of the tuft in her teeth while she swallowed the part already chewed to be saved as cud — rank grass, green and succulent to see, transmuted into fresh milk in her mind, mouthfuls of it swallowed down in delight. Once she gripped a green stalk of it hanging from the cow's mouth, but the animal's teeth were too dourly clenched on it, she let go of it again not bothering any more.

—Dadda.

No, she wouldn't take her hand off the cow's haunch, the youngster had to tug at her apron before her eyes fixed on him. Dadda. Words coming in short gasps, overcome with fright and hurry. Out in the byre. The halters, they're round his neck. Swinging from the beam, eyes turned up in his head. Mamma. Mamma. Home, quick, quick.

—Good boy . . . swinging from the beam . . .

The words sparked life in the depth of her mind as the carbrakes had done a while ago. She stood still . . . She realised then she was driving the cow down to the Shore Garth as she did every morning. In a little while she tapped the cow again — it was easier to go on. Light as cobwebs in a dark room waving under a breath of wind the fabric of her thoughts wavered while she kept in step with the slow cow, going on . . .